Can I Tell You a Story?

By Michael Austin Miller

Can I Tell You a Story?

DEDICATION

Many of these stories have been written with the goal of making two people laugh;
my brother and sister, Timothy Miller and Susan Still.

Not only are they two of my favorite and most important people in my life, they are often central figures in several of these stories.

They've inspired me to write and along the way, they've reminded me of details and have offered feedback. In some cases, they've contributed entire scenes.

Because there are no other people on this earth with whom I've shared as many laughs, it is with great joy that I dedicate this book to them.

ACKNOWLEDGMENTS

Thank you to all who've encouraged me to tell and write stories over the years. It means so much to know that people take the time to read them, reflect, and often share their thoughts with me.

I offer tremendous thanks to:

...Nicole Miller, Tim's wife, and Joey Still, Susan's husband, for joining the Miller clan and adding to it.

...my nephews and nieces: Timothy Miller, Donna Claire Still, Sullivan Still, & Emily Miller.

...my dad and step-mother, Mike and Teresa Miller.

...my grandparents, aunts, uncles, and cousins.

...the person who taught me to love words and constantly reminded me to never underestimate the power of the pen, my mother, Donna Fletcher Miller, who passed away in 2001 and without whom none of these stories would have been possible.

...my former English Teachers who taught me to love creative writing, many of whom have recently encouraged me - via social media - to continue this endeavor: Mrs. Wanda Chamber, Mrs. Julie McIntosh Stephenson, Mrs. Linda Page Vaughan, Mrs. Kathy Schwalbe, Mrs. Kay Metzger-Merkel, and Dr. Debra Boyd.

...my tribe - the people who've listened to or who've read these stories in order to give helpful feedback or who have encouraged me along the way: Stephen Marshall-Ward, Kerri Rundle, and Beth Hamlin.

...Stephanie Harris and Juris Zommers for their help editing this book.

* * *

...my best friend, Kevin Gray, who heard most of these stories over the phone before anyone else.

...my partner, Brian, for the wonderful life we share, his support, encouragement, and for constantly making me laugh.

...my dog, Brutus, who sat below me as I typed. He heard me read these stories aloud so many times that he could probably tell them. He seemed a bit reluctant to give me much constructive feedback but sometimes all one needs is a listening ear - even though he was sleeping most of the time.

INTRODUCTION

You were probably amazed that I could come up with such a clever and witty title for this book.

If you're around me often, you know that in nearly every interaction, you'll hear me say, "Can I tell you a story?," at least once.

I can't help it. I love telling stories. I have so many true stories and there's nothing quite as fun as "spinning a yarn."

About a year ago, I had an "Ah ha" moment when a friend asked me, 'Do you think you pursued the positions you've held because they've each given you a platform from which to tell your stories?'

Instantly, I could see the truth: I wanted to be a teacher so I could tell stories to my students. I wanted to conduct music ensembles so I could tell stories in my rehearsals. I wanted to serve churches so I could tell stories about faith and all things Divine as often as possible.

Stories are treasures.

We learn about ourselves and our place in this world by the stories we hear, the stories we retell, the stories we craft and share, but most importantly, the stories we tell ourselves *about* ourselves.

* * *

While most of the stories in this book are funny tales of actual events that have been heavily embellished, in the third section of the book you'll find stories about the events surrounding my mother's passing. They are absolutely true. They each point to The Divine and these aren't stories that I experienced alone. In each one, others were present, and they've read these stories prior to publication in order to validate them.

As you read these stories, it is my deepest hope that you'll experience an occasional chuckle, chill, or tear.

ABOUT THE SAND DOLLARS

When I think about my childhood, so many things flood my mind, but one thing - one symbol - stands out above the rest: the Sand Dollar.

My family spent many summer days on Sullivan's Island or the Isle of Palms combing the ocean floor with our feet searching for those flat shelled burrowing sea urchins with their odd, fuzzy, velvety exterior.

My mother had a great love for them. For several years, our Christmas Tree was lit with clear lights and covered by bright white Sand Dollars. Those trees were simple but beautiful. Over the years, my mom gave countless Sand Dollars as gifts to friends and family.

When my brother was married, wedding-goers received an envelope containing a Sand Dollar and a copy of the *Legend of the Sand Dollar* poem. The author is unknown, but you can easily find the poem online

* * *

Sand Dollars also hold a solemn meaning for my family and me. Before my mother's casket was closed for the final time, Dad, Susan, Tim, Nicole, and I each placed a Sand Dollar - five in total - in the casket with her. Since she is a part of many of these stories, I used Sand Dollars throughout the book as a simple but beautiful sign of remembrance.

TABLE OF CONTENTS

Michael Austin Miller

* * *

PART THREE: MOM

PART FOUR: SMALL TOWN LIVIN'

PART FIVE: GOD WINKS

PART ONE

Family Time

CHAPTER ONE

Music at the Millers'

After my final college voice recital, my voice teacher complimented my performance in front of my parents. It felt so good to hear such affirming words. After all, upon first hearing me sing, my teacher said, "Your voice reminds me of Mel Tormé, but not in a good way... your nickname should be The Velvet SMOG."

Hearing my teacher's compliment, my father chimed in, "I can hardly play the radio."

While I might be the only person in my immediate family who is a career musician, Dad...actually, my entire family...LOVES music...Classical Music. Dad used to brag to everyone about how he constantly exposed us kids to the Classics.

That's right...Dad played Ray Charles' *Hit the Road Jack* among many other classics on the record player all the time, and Mom wore the grooves off her recording of Gladys Knight's *Midnight Train to Georgia*.

In our house, music wasn't just for enjoyment or entertainment...it was also educational. My father taught us history through song. To this day, he can still do a mean *Battle of New Orleans*. I can almost hear him now.

And Dad loves to dance. My dad had...I mean HAS...all the moves. Yes, he does! ...Every...single... one. He has 'em all.

He once told me that the Band Director at Beaufort High School, where he went to school, wouldn't even let him play cymbals in the marching band.

I explained to Dad that his social standing in the Beaufort community might have intimidated the band director.

You see, I come from royalty. It is true. My dad was the self-proclaimed *Duke of Beaufort*. I tried to be the *Duke of Goose Creek* but that title never sounded quite as sophisticated.

In all seriousness, I've been thinking about the influence my parents had on me...personally and musically. The fact that they were opposites in nearly every way is the reason I am so well-rounded...I guess.

My mother was a "Southern Belle," but give her a Gin and Tonic and she'd sing her college *Alma Mater* all night long.

Give her some Goldschlager and she became a Kung Fu Ninja Warrior. I once saw her take down a grown man who stood over 6-feet tall in the middle of his own living room at a Christmas party. She then leg-wrestled him until he tapped out. When she was done, she stood up, brushed herself off, gave a tribal yell, threw some of their Christmas presents into the fireplace, and then threatened to take on anyone else who might want to fight…but I digress.

Back to the music: my dad's belief that he had no musical talent was wrong all along. Both of my parents were musical.

My mom loved music and she loved to sing - especially old church hymns. She'd often get so emotional in church that she would just lip sync the words. The more moving the song, the softer she sang. You knew she really loved a song if you couldn't hear her singing at all…but visually, she appeared to be all-in. She was the original Milli Vanilli.

What my Dad lacks in musical talent he more than makes up for with volume and enthusiasm. The more he likes a song the louder he sings and the more he dances.

I am sincerely grateful to both of them for showing me what music is really all about and for teaching me something that isn't often taught in a music courses: the power of music to uplift, inspire, and move the human spirit.

CHAPTER TWO

The Table

There have been very few Sundays in my life when I've not been in church. Most often, my absences have been because I was out of town doing other music events such as concerts.

I estimate that since 1994 - when I became a professional church musician - I've missed maybe 15 Sundays simply because I was too ill to fulfill my responsibilities.

There have been numerous Sundays when I should have stayed home but went to church anyway. Today is not one of those.

Today, it is abundantly clear that I could not do my job even if I had the energy to get there.

In addition to regular Sunday services, Church is where we celebrate Weddings, Births, Baptisms, First Communions, Confirmations, Graduations, Engagements and a whole host of other events. It is also the place where we honor the dead and commend their spirits to God and into God's eternal care.

It is where we gather with family, friends, friends who have become our family, neighbors, and strangers.

It is where we see what unites us…where we are One-in-Spirit.

The Church is where we lift our voices, our bodies, our hearts, and our minds to God who has created all things as an offering in response to all we've been given.

If you're like me, it is part of your week's routine. It is just one of our weekly rituals of which there are many (most of which go unrecognized as such), but it isn't the same as conditioning your hair every other day. For me, if I miss this ritual, my week doesn't feel right.

It isn't too unlike the mealtime ritual my family had when I was a boy. We ate most dinners together. Not doing so was a rare exception - even during the busiest seasons of life.

After a long day, we kids had chores: cleaning the morning dishes, taking out the trash, and picking up pinecones in the yard.

My dad was obsessed with having a pinecone-free yard. He'd rather have three-days worth of garbage piled up in the kitchen than see a pinecone in the yard.

Do you have any idea how hard that is to maintain? We had 21 pine trees in our back yard alone and at least 5 in the front. The only blessing of *Hurricane Hugo* was that we lost about 1/3 of those trees. Still, every afternoon - come rain or come shine - one of us was picking up those damn pinecones.

Mom and Dad would prepare the meal - sometimes with the assistance of one of the kids. As they did, they'd socialize, debrief on their day, tell stories, and laugh.

One of the three of us kids would set the table. This in itself was a ritual because mom was very particular about how she wanted the napkins folded, where they were placed and how the tablecloth or placemats, plates, bowls, forks, knives, and spoons were to be set - as well as the salt and pepper shakers. Most of the time, a candle would be lit, too.

It was the duty of the table-setter to know what meal was being prepared in order to put out the proper condiments; salad dressing, ketchup, etc.

Oh yeah…and don't forget to turn off the television - we were never allowed to watch TV during dinner.

After dinner, someone had to clear and clean the table, and one or two of us had to wash and dry the dishes.

During the meal, we'd all sit down at the same time - in the same assigned seats - around an old, round, sturdy, simple, and beautiful pedestal table. It was the perfect size for the space and the size of our family. It was the centerpiece that made our house our home.

We'd hold hands and say two blessings.

Whoever started the prayers determined which of the two we'd say first.

"Bless us, O Lord, and these thy gifts which we are about to receive from thy bounty, through Christ, Our Lord. Amen."

Immediately following:

"Come, Lord Jesus, our guest to be and blest these gifts bestowed by thee."

Mom would almost always follow up with an additional prayer said in matching cadence "and bless

Susan during her tournament." and we'd all say a robust "Amen."

Later, we added the second verse to that second prayer:

"And bless our friends everywhere and keep them in thy loving care. Amen."

Mom would use this time to teach etiquette: "If you're eating a fine meal of chicken, you mustn't use your hands. Use your fork and knife like this..." Sometimes, she'd read something to us that she'd found inspirational.

My dad instituted a rule that everyone could say "anything they wanted" at that table. I don't think he really meant "anything," but the idea was that there was freedom to speak our mind as we sat in a circle with our tribe in the comfort of our home and around that table.

That was where many arguments were had, many stories were told, many card or board games were played, and countless meals were shared.

Many severe and solemn conversations were had there, too, and so were birthday parties, baby showers, and neighborhood gatherings.

More than meals, *laughter* is what I most associate with being at that table.

I am sure that this wasn't unique to just the Miller kids, but it was often our goal to create as much fun as possible at the table, and it didn't take much to get a laugh.

My parents taught us to laugh. What a gift. They loved telling each other stories that made the other laugh. They both possessed a quick wit though my mother's was more reserved.

Of course, we kids loved making each other laugh, but that wasn't the goal at the dinner table. Our goal was to get our parents laughing. It wasn't uncommon for things to get out of control, and sometimes a simple snicker would instigate a raucous outburst.

We always walked a fine line, though.

If all we did was make our siblings laugh while our parents looked at us disapprovingly, it wasn't uncommon for my dad to say, "Ok now, you're letting the jerks get hold of you" (I still don't know exactly what that meant but it implied "STOP before someone is forcibly removed from the table").

Sometimes though, he was playing the supporting role to mom's disapproval, but we knew he wanted to laugh because we saw his struggle to keep a straight face.

No matter if there had been discord among us, there was a commitment to each other to come together at our table, to put those issues aside, and to enjoy being together. Even on days when we'd upset our parents and were sent to our room, we always knew that we were welcome at the table.

I can't remember the stories that were told or what we laughed about, but I remember the spirit of the dinner ritual, the traditions, and I remember how I felt sitting there.

I remember feeling like the five of us - no matter what our day had held - we were one-in-spirit.

That table - where we broke bread as a family each

night - held so many fond memories that when I finally had a place of my own, I tracked down a table that nearly matched my family's. It took years to find, but it became the centerpiece that made my house feel like home.

Thinking of my family's mealtime ritual reminds me of the church. Without the family gathering around our table regularly, the week wouldn't seem right.

Over the years, I've attended at least 3000 services - most of which I've helped lead. I can't remember all sermons, the songs, or events, but I remember the spirit of the ritual, and the traditions, and I remember how I felt sitting in each church. I can remember feeling like all of us - no matter our background - were one-in-spirit.

CHAPTER THREE

A Cherry Hill Halloween

Like so many kids, we Millers loved Halloween, but no one loved it as much as my brother, Tim.

For a few years, he turned our garage into a Haunted House where the only way people could get candy was to subject themselves to the horrors that awaited behind that thin sheet of black plastic that separated the living from the undead.

The garage, which he had draped in black plastic, was illuminated by a strobe light.

One boombox played Heavy Metal while another across the garage played "horror sounds."

He had an entire cast of friends decked out in some of the scariest masks you've ever seen.

Some jumped out at people, someone used a leaf blower, another used a chain-less chainsaw, we cranked up the lawnmower and the weed wacker a few times before mom decided that they might be too dangerous...and we all screamed...but no one screamed louder than my mom.

I had never been so proud of my mom as I was that night.

Honestly, she should have won an *Academy Award* for her portrayal of a scared, dying woman on a mad scientist's lab table (an old desk).

"Help Me! Help Me!" she bellowed in a blood-curdling scream for several hours. She was creepier than Kathy Bates.

I think my sister, Susan, was the "mad scientist" but my recollection is a bit foggy.

I dug a full-length grave in the backyard. It was only about three feet deep but since the task was utterly exhausting, that was all I was willing to do.

I spent much of the night jumping out of that hole and wishing that it wasn't so deep. By the end of the night, my legs were so tired that I couldn't even crouch down and pop up. About the best I could do was stand waist deep in the hole, no longer wearing that hot mask, fearing the onset of heatstroke, and mopping up my sweaty brow with my flannel shirt while panting and half-heartedly shouting "boo..?.."

I have no idea how many people went through the Miller's *Maze of Terror*, but there was a line out to the street.

At times, we - the cast - laughed so hard that we were crying. Of course, some kids left crying and will be forever traumatized by the gruesome and jarring experience.

One of the highlights, however, was that I met - for the first time - the love of Tim's life, Nicole. I'd heard about her from Tim, Mom, Dad, and Susan.

Tim was totally taken by her....writing love letters, leaving flowers on her car so she'd get them after work. Smitten is not a strong enough word, and I know that he feels the same way or more so all of these years later.

I loved Nicole from the moment I met her. After all, anyone who'd be willing to jump right in, throw on a mask, and join we Millers in screaming at a whole bunch of scared little kids, most of whom we didn't even know, is alright in my book!

CHAPTER FOUR

Christmas Morning

Christmas - the most wonderful time of the year.

That was certainly true when I was a kid. It was filled with awe and wonder...and a little fear, too, if I am honest.

I was one of those kids who was a little freaked out by the idea of a man - Santa - sneaking into our house on Christmas Eve, and I certainly didn't like sitting on his lap.

Worse still, we didn't have a chimney so my parents - in their infinite wisdom - told me that Santa would sneak in through our living room window.

For the next few years, all I wanted for Christmas was security bars installed over every possible entry to our house.

Like all kids, we loved decorating our Christmas Tree. There were a few years where I think we had the most stunning tree in the whole world.

Over the summer, our parents took us to the beach (which was something we did often as kids) where we

Can I Tell You a Story?

collected Sand Dollars. Later, we bleached them, painted them white, and lacquered them. When Christmas time came, we decorated the tree with white lights and the bright white sand dollars that were tied to the boughs of the tree with red silk ribbon.

I miss that time; the wonder...the innocence of childhood...the belief in the unbelievable...and the presents.

One Christmas morning, my brother and I found pocket knives in our stockings. With the skills of a ninja, my brother and I used our knives to assist in opening all of our presents.

When we were almost finished opening presents, there were three presents left; one for each of the three of us. Since they were all the same size, our folks wanted us to open them at the same time.

When given the "go ahead," my brother and I began slashing the wrapping paper off the boxes. My sister, on the other hand, was far more deliberate. She even took the time to read aloud the warnings on the outside of the box just as my brother and I plunged our knives into our boxes...

"Do not open with sharp objects."

My brother and I did not read the warnings emblazoned in large red letters, nor did we see the image of a box cutter covered by a large "X" on each side of the box.

It was too late.

As we pulled the box flaps apart, we were both

greeted with white polyester fiber that slowly expanded - kind of like one of those prank nut cans that surprise the opener with a snake that springs out when the lid is lifted...or a baking soda and vinegar volcano.

Our mom stormed out of the room in fury, "We can't give you boys anything nice," while my sister - who had gently opened her gift - was wrapping herself in a beautiful burgundy sleeping bag.

My brother and I had destroyed those sleeping bags, and we destroyed my parents master plan.

You see, we were going on a trip where the three of us would have to sleep on the floor - in sleeping bags.

Before we left, my mother tried to patch our bags the best she could. We packed for the trip and strapped all three of those sleeping bags to the roof of our minivan and began our the trek.

The tension was so high in the car that my parents were chewing Xanax like they were Chicklets. No one spoke for nearly two hours...actually no one spoke until we were pulled over by what we thought was a police officer, but it was just a nice man in a Crown Victoria:

"Did you have two sleeping bags on your roof?" he asked.

"Yes," my dad said.

"You dropped them about a mile back."

Wouldn't you know - the two bags that had been slashed had somehow flown off the roof of the car.

My dad got out, tightened the remaining sleep bag to

the roof, and we circled back. We drove and drove but those sleeping bags were nowhere to be found.

More frustrated than ever, we resumed our trip. My dad was driving like a mad-man. Silence was always the best course of action in such situations.

About five minutes later, as we sped along the highway, we heard a sound up on the rooftop…and it wasn't Santa. It was a loud fluttering sound and then something popped.

Suddenly, we all turned around and saw a blur of burgundy as Susan's sleeping bag went flying away at 75 miles per hour. As it did, it somehow opened up - completely- and landed splayed out across the highway.

Dad slammed on the brakes.

We all jumped out of the minivan - like we were the *A-team* or something - and ran toward the bag. It was like we were in slow motion - running and waving our arms, shaking our heads, and yelling,

"NnnnnOooooooooooooo!"

…as a mack truck and 17 other vehicles ran over that bag. That poor bag was tossed to and fro as each car paraded over it.

Once the cars had passed and the show was over, my dad disgustedly grabbed the bag, balled it up and hastily threw it in the back seat.

When it comes to nearly having a psychotic break over the holidays, my dad was the original Clark Griswold. If the tension in the car had been bad before, it escalated even more, and no one dared to say a word…until my sister - who was, perhaps, the only one who could have spoken since she was my dad's princess

- broke the silence about five minutes later, "Um...I'm not sleeping in it."

With that, the tension was broken and we all laughed until we were in tears; good tears.

That Christmas memory will live on forever thanks to those knives and those sleeping bags.

It ranks right up there with the time my brother was in charge of hanging the lights on our tree. Apparently, he hung them twice. The first time, my mother critiqued his work saying, "Timothy, put some of the lights deeper in the tree - closer to the trunk - so that it looks full and bright." On his second attempt, he wrapped 57,400 white lights around the trunk of the tree causing the tree to look like it had a nuclear core.

That night, with the lights still plugged into the power outlet, my mother cut all of the lights off the trunk of the tree with pinking sheers while the rest of us watched in silent, wide-eyed amazement...and no one dared to stop her or even say a word.

Good times...and Merry Christmas!!

CHAPTER FIVE

Miracles

In 1994, I witnessed something in church that I'll never forget!

While the pastor was praying, he began coughing uncontrollably and so violently that everyone opened their eyes. He looked distressed as he clutched his throat and seemed to writhe in pain. Not knowing why he was suddenly behaving so erratically, everyone simultaneously jumped to the only logical conclusion: he must be possessed!

Four-letter words streamed out his mouth as he dashed to the Baptismal Font where he poured the entire basin of holy water over his face while guzzling all the liquid holiness he could.

Seeing him corrupt the baptismal waters, the church members became unglued, and they instantly seemed possessed, too - kicking over chairs, jumping up on pews, slapping each other, and recklessly hollering "Get behind thee, Satan!" to anyone and everyone around.

As one man grabbed a fire extinguisher and sprayed it over the unruly crowd, the pastor's wife became hysterical and began chasing her husband out of the church while throwing a vase with the church's twenty-seven-year-old faux-silk flower arrangement. I will never forget the terror in her voice as she repeatedly screamed: "The power of Christ compels you! The power of Christ compels you!"

Everyone joined in chasing him out of the church as they hurled whatever they could grab; hymnals, bibles, purses, offering plates, envelopes, a flagpole, a few candles, the artificial Christmas Tree, and at least two pairs of dentures.

Had we known he had just swallowed a fly, we might have gone easier on him.

As a church musician for over two decades, I have accumulated a large collection of equally memorable experiences. For instance: one Ash Wednesday, a little girl heard the pastor say, "We are but dust and to dust we shall return," and interrupted the service by asking her father in a sweet but loud voice, "Dad, what is butt dust?"

But…there is one memory that surpasses all others.

It happened during a friend's wedding for which my sister, Susan, was asked to read the couple's favorite scripture verses.

As she approached the pulpit, the minister offered her a microphone, but she waved it out of her face and shot him a look that seemed to say, *beat it, old man!*, but she then smiled kindly and said, "No thanks. I'm a teacher."

She turned to the congregation and in a somewhat

meek voice asked, "Can you hear me?" The group nodded in affirmation and offered a few hushed yeses.

The minister insistently offered her the mic again, but Susan recoiled and shot him another look that seemed to say, *Get that thing out of my face...right now!...please.*

She unceremoniously curled the paper she was holding into a megaphone and putting it to her mouth as if she was leading a cheer at a high school pep rally, she shouted, "I said, can you heeeaaaarrrrr meeee?"

As she stretched out the words "heeeaaaarrrrr meeee," she was so loud that she altered the atmospheric pressure in the room and everyone felt their ears pop due to the drastic change.

A bit stunned, the congregation laughed uncomfortably and retaliated with an equally loud, "YESSSSSS!!!!!!!"

She took a deep breath and in a volume comparable to 32 bagpipers playing *Scotland the Brave,* she read, "If I speak in the tongues of men or of angels, but do not have love, I am only a resounding gong or a clanging cymbal."

Based on the way people were thrown against the back of their pews, her voice was louder than any resounding gong or cymbal they'd ever heard! Nearly everyone looked wind-blown, but those who sat in the direct line of her tsunami of sound looked as if they had been sitting behind the engines of a Boeing 747.

Some would later claim that she had given them whiplash, some claimed that their eardrums had hemorrhaged a bit, and some said they had a temporary loss of appetite - which has yet to be explained.

When Susan was a child, she knew she had a gift but chose to keep it a secret until one fateful night.

She was in second grade when she volunteered to be a *carnival barker* for the school's annual *Fall Bazaar*.

All night long you could hear voice resonating throughout the entire school, and the floor trembled a bit each time she yelled, "Step right up, and I'll guess your weight and age!"

Not only were people amazed by her volume, but she had the uncanny ability to guess people's exact weight and age.

Susan enjoyed this new-found attention and began to guess *everyone's* weight and age whether they were at her booth or not.

When teachers walked by she'd make a big production, "And now, Ladies and Gentlemen, we have Ms. Little. Weight 212. Age 54."

Seeing a cute seven-year-old doing that was hilarious at first, but soon women began avoiding her at all costs.

To this day, she is still more accurate than most scales, and occasionally - if she's had a drink or two - she'll yell out people's weight at the most inappropriate times; at the mall, sporting events, funerals, or during school staff meetings.

I once took her to see *Beauty and the Beast on Ice*. She hollered every cast member's weight as they made their first appearance on the ice. Susan had us both in stitches. The cast members were less than amused, but the audience seemed to egg her on...except for one large man who shushed her...to which she curtly replied, "Shut it, 347."

Reminiscing about this reminds me of how much I've missed my family since moving to the Northwest. Fortunately, every now and then, if the breeze is just right, I can hear Susan's voice floating on the wind as she calls her kids inside for dinner, and that is particularly nice now that we're 3000 miles apart.

Back to the story: As Susan continued to read the scripture, her voice seemed to thrash the wedding-goers wildly about the face and neck, and the groom's grandfather responded by growing physically agitated.

I'd imagine he was in his late 80s (Susan would know for sure), and based on the number of times he yelled "what?" as he was ushered to his seat before the wedding, he was stone-cold deaf.

Unbeknownst to all assembled, something significant was happening as she read...something very special. Susan could feel the Spirit moving and couldn't help but crank up the volume. She took on the likeness of a holy-rolling preacher. Heck, she was preachin', and people loved it!!

Suddenly, with the agility of a teenager - and to everyone's amazement - the groom's grandfather jumped up from his seat and proclaimed with a sense of reckless abandon, "God Almighty, she's loud...but Hallelujah! I can hear again!!"

Everyone could feel his joy and excitement as he carried on: "I've been healed! I can hear again!!"

Now filled with vim and vigor, he ran up to the pulpit and hugged Susan. The congregation rose to their feet in thunderous applause.

People started shoutin', and praisin', and singin'! Others went up front to thank Susan for the miraculous healings they too had received.

As folks settled down, one of the gentlemen whose hearing had been restored asked, "Now that I can hear, can you do anything about how much my wife talks?"

The wedding continued, the couple was wed, the families were thrilled, and most were still a little dazed and confused as Susan's voice continued to ring in their ears.

After the service, people were still gathering their wits about them as they made their way to the Fellowship Hall for the Reception.

Along the way, someone noticed something odd in the cemetery. Above every grave, the ground looked disturbed, and there was loose dirt everywhere.

We all figured that Susan had been on the verge of raising the dead. She must have stopped just in time. Had she kept reading, there's a good chance she might have raised those bodies all the way up!

Susan has since married and now has kids. She swears that her husband, kids, and their dogs are the only beings on earth incapable of hearing her.

Whether it is the pastor and the fly, butt dust, or the wedding-day miracle, stories such as these have raised my spirits through the power of humor. I hope you've had a good chuckle or two, too.

Can I Tell You a Story?

CHAPTER SIX

A Janis Joplin Christmas

Here's a little-known fact about my sister, Susan: during her last two years of college and the first few years of teaching, she supplemented her income as a Janis Joplin impersonator.

People who know Susan might be inclined to think that I am embellishing or making this up. I know...because it *IS* hard to imagine a person as calm, quiet and reserved as Susan assuming the likeness of someone like Janis, but it is true.

Now, you must also know that she kept this a secret from the family for years...until one Christmas Day.

Most of the family was gathered in our living room with my mom's mom, my dad's dad, my aunt, uncle, and cousins, and a few other innocent bystanders.

We had eaten dinner and opened presents and were sitting back enjoying the glow of the Christmas Tree, the fire in the fireplace, and the breeze that whipped through the house since every single window and door was wide open, and every fan was on full blast.

Yes, my friends, that's how you do Christmas in the

low country of South Carolina. You light a fire on Christmas Day even if it is a mild and sunny 74-degrees outside.

The music from the CD player that had played all day seemed to grow a bit louder - only because we were all settling down and beginning to experience the onset of the traditional food coma; everyone except Susan. Somehow, she still had energy and was in the kitchen cleaning dishes.

As we sat there with our bellies full and our eyes half-shut, we heard the CD carousel switch from Andy Williams singing *It's the Most Wonderful Time of the Year* to a new CD and the iconic and very familiar acoustic guitar introduction of Janis Joplin's famous song, *Me & Bobby McGee.*

Apparently, not all five of the CDs in the cd carousel were Christmas-oriented, but no one seemed to mind.

Like the sound of a snake charmer's flute, Susan seemed to be lured out of the kitchen and into the living room. The song seemed to have her under some kind of hypnotic spell.

It was then that, for the first time, she decided to show everyone her truth - a truth she had hidden for so many years, and she began to sing.

Susan grabbed the stereo remote, cranked the volume all the way up, and then used the remote as a makeshift microphone.

A couple of family members thought that she was inviting everyone to sing along until Susan shot them a stink-eye and yelled into the microphone "Shut it!"

While people all over the world were smiling in response to the joy of Christmas, we all smiled awkwardly at the spectacle of Susan's hips gyrating - a sultry movement that became a little more aggressive with every beat of the song.

By the time she finally got to the chorus, she was in full-speed, and she yelled into the arena-sized crowd of 15, "Now, here's a Christmas present you'll never forget," and with a violent thrust of her hips toward Grandpa, she continued.

On she sang, on she danced, and on she entertained.

Realizing that we were more or less being held hostage by her performance, we all loosened up and Grandma, who had had enough eggnog for a busload of British tourists, began to resume consciousness - shaking her head and shoulders back-and-fourth in rhythm with the song.

Mom, who sat closest to Susan, grabbed my sister's hand and gently tapped it as she mouthed the words, "that's enough."

Susan shook her hand out mom's and jumped onto the hearth of the fireplace where her shadow cast from the fire seemed to shimmy and shake all over the room.

Grandpa even started tapping his toes.

It was fun and to be perfectly honest, Susan's performance was spot-on.

All those years Susan spent smoking cigars back in high school were really paying off because her raspy voice was perfect.

To be clear, this wasn't just an alcohol-fueled karaoke

rendition of the song. Susan WAS Janis!

The only one not enjoying the show was our mom who looked mortified.

Finally, mom ever so gently walked across the room to the hearth, smiled at everyone apologetically, put her arm behind Susan, and whispered something into her ear.

With a look of confusion, Susan said into the microphone, "No...I'm not embarrassing myself!"

Susan was unfazed and in the spirit of a rockstar, she picked up a few of Dad's brand new golf clubs and began strumming them like a guitar.

Susan was amazing. Soon, everyone was clapping along - even mom.

As the song wound down, Susan seemed to regain composure - almost like she didn't know what she had been doing. It was strange - in an exorcism sort of way.

On the last strum of the guitar, Susan did a mic-drop and the batteries from the remote went flying.

Mom tried to escort Susan out of the living room to have a "conference," but before they were out of the room, the song, *Take Another Piece of My Heart* came on.

Susan broke away and once again took center stage, but before she could really get into character, mom ran over to the stereo and yanked its electric cord from the wall with such force that the cord broke - leaving just the plug in the wall and the wire in mom's hand.

Everyone had a good laugh and things calmed down.

* * *

Susan no longer does her Janis show - which is a shame because she was so darn good.

She did return to the "stage" twice since then.

Once, she attended a party with me at the SC's Governor's Mansion. When the Governor asked Susan what she did, the few glasses of wine I had made me blurt out that she was a Janis impersonator which, of course, caused him to ask her to demonstrate. There, with SC dignitaries everywhere, she broke out into an a cappella rendition. People were stunned, and the Security Agents were alarmed - to say the least.

The second time was at her wedding reception when some cousins who were present that Christmas years before had the D.J. play the song. After only hearing the first three beats of the song, Susan once again transformed into Janis - in a wedding dress. It was quite a display.

She now spends her time and attention on her family and on teaching, but she'll always be able to look back on that day and say, "I gave them a Christmas present they'll never forget."

...and let's face it - not every person can make such a statement with that much certainty.

CHAPTER SEVEN

Fight or Flight

In case you've never stepped on a snake, I don't recommend it. I was only about seven or eight years old when it happened to me.

I was running barefoot across a field at *Charlestown Landing* when I caught sight of something out of my peripheral vision.

In a split second, I saw it, and it saw me.

We tried to avoid each other but because neither of us knew which way the other was going, we ended up crossing paths with my right foot landing on a Black Racer.

In my memory, it was 15-feet long but was probably closer to 5-feet.

The body's *Fight or Flight Response* is powerful. I am sure my reaction resembled what you'd see in a movie when someone encounters an explosion and is thrown back through the air by the blast.

Nowadays, I often see Garter Snakes in the shrubbery around our yard and even though I know they pose no threat, I'm often caught off-guard and usually jump back a few feet before I even know why.

I am not proud of this, but in most cases that reaction is accompanied with an involuntary string of one-syllable, percussive expletives that I refuse to write and are better left to your imagination.

Thankfully, this sometimes burdensome involuntary *Fight or Flight Response* has saved many lives.

When my siblings and I were kids, we spent nearly every *Fourth of July* at my paternal grandparent's house on the Pungo River in Belhaven, NC.

One day, after all the adult men had returned from Golf, everyone was in the backyard either playing or watching the annual *Miller Invitational Wiffle T-Ball Classic*. I believe it was the Championship or as my Grandpa would say in his hard, gravelly Boston-ish accent: the "Cham-PEEN-chip"

My sister, Susan, was at bat and my cousin, Tyler, was on deck.

I wasn't playing that day.

Don't be fooled by my athletic, muscular, overtly masculine physique and chiseled features. I am not nearly as athletically inclined as I look. I have been benching myself during Miller sporting events ever since the Christmas when I had to jump in the river to retrieve the football I missed when someone pity-tossed it to me.

A "pity-toss" is when someone feels sorry for you because you're so incredibly inept to make you feel good about yourself. They lightly toss the ball to you from three feet away thinking there'd be no way you could miss it.

I missed it. Of course I did...and did I mention it was Christmas? That water was freezing.

Back to the July Fourth Cham-PEEN-chip Whiffle ball game:

Just as Susan went to swing, Dad, who was on the mound, went into fight or flight mode.

A Water Moccasin that had apparently been in the nearby shrubs was heading straight for Susan and Ty.

These poisonous water snakes are known to be aggressive because, instead of fleeing when humans are around, they'll stand their ground and strike if threatened.

By the time Dad reached Susan and Ty, the snake was a mere two feet away from the kids. Dad grabbed the bat and swung at the snake sending it soaring across the yard. Dad ran after it and began beating the hell out of that snake.

Granny, too, went into fight or flight mode and grabbed a garden hoe.

From fifteen yards away, she hurled that hoe across the yard with the precision of an Olympic Javelin Thrower. When it landed, its blade severed the snake just behind its head.

Actually, she didn't really throw the hoe - I added that for the dramatic effect.

Regardless, she grabbed the hoe and ran toward the snake with the speed of Jackie Joyner-Kersee, and within a matter of seconds that snake was dead.

Everyone was fleeing the area as aunts and uncles

yelled, "get back," "get away," "stay away from the head, it can still bite you."

Granny, who acted like killing a venomous snake was an everyday occurrence, began tossing the remains into the river. We kids gathered at the bulkhead to watch as crabs started feasting. Understandably, that experience made the idea of an afternoon swim seem less appealing.

My mother was able to control her fight or flight response pretty well - unless she saw a cockroach. In that case, she'd release a primal, blood-curdling scream that would make you think that she had stumbled upon a dead body. It was very unsettling and it wasn't uncommon for her to spray an entire can of roach kill on a cockroach she'd find outside in the back corner of our yard - so imagine what she'd do if she saw one in the house!

Unlike others whose fight or flight response lasts a few seconds, Mom's would last an hour - at least.

Anytime we'd go to an outdoor event, Mom suited up in what she called her "arsenal" and was on high alert.

I kid you not, she'd have a fly swatter and a whiffle ball bat locked and loaded in a pistol holster strapped to her torso, and she'd wear a fully loaded tool belt she had personally engineered to carry 12 cans of Black Flag Roach Spray. She wore that stuff to every outdoor concert, baseball game, during her daily walk around the neighborhood, and when she volunteered as a crossing guard. She didn't mind people staring because she knew that they'd wish they were as well prepared in the event of a cockroach apocalypse of Biblical proportion.

One night, Mom was walking into our living room where the rest of the family was watching tv when she erupted in that horrifying scream.

She dashed into the living room, did a few ranger rolls and an army crawl until she got to the dining room. There, she did a series of cartwheels into the laundry room and out to the garage where she stored a pallet of Black Flag spray.

Over the years, she had mastered these tactical escape maneuvers but that night she was clumsier than usual - knocking pictures off the wall and kicking the birdcage.

Poor Pebbles, our Australian Finch, was peeping with all her might - suspended with one claw gripping the cage and the other gripping the swing that swung violently.

When Mom reentered the living room, she did so using the ceiling's wood beams as monkey bars. I still don't know how she managed to do that while holding a can of Black Flag in each hand.

She landed right in front of the roach and with a loud, "Gotcha," and started spraying.

She sprayed and sprayed while the rest of us were coughing and gasping for air.

Soon, she had exhausted the first can. Not only was she out of spray, we were also out of breathable oxygen and had to run outside.

Maybe it was the influence of the vapors, but Dad panicked, picked up a log that was sitting beside the fireplace, and threw it through one of the back windows. I still don't know if he thought he could escape that way or if he did that for ventilation.

Soon, all of us except mom were standing in the front yard peering through the door to see what was happening.

That cockroach had been dead for at least 5 minutes before she stopped spraying but she wouldn't stop running around the inside of the house yelling - which sounded like a fire alarm going off in our house.

Mom was unrelenting. Occasionally, you'd hear things crashing - like the china in the china hutch, and something repeatedly hit a whole cluster of notes the piano really hard - like she was jumping up and down on its keys.

Finally, Dad ran into the house and took her out of the fumes with a one-shoulder Fireman's Carry.

All of the excitement drew neighbors from their houses, and people driving by pulled over to offer assistance. To a passerby, it would have appeared that we were watching our house burn down but there was no fire - just enough fumes billowing from the front door that it looked like smoke.

My dad kept yelling, "Nobody light a match!"

Do you know what "Nobody light a match" sounds like to an eighth-grader? It sounds like: "Michael, light a match. Go light a match right now." All I could think about doing was lighting a match.

***

After a few hours, my dad deemed the house safe enough for us to reenter. We slept with all the windows open that night and every fan on high.

By the next morning, we'd almost forgotten about the previous night's excitement. I don't remember what year it was, but it was the morning of April 17th - my mother's and my brother's birthday.

Mom was calm, cool, and collected as she sat at the dining room table doing what she did every morning - reading the obituaries. That was her way to start every day off right because as long as you don't see your own name listed, you're probably okay.

My brother, sister, and I sat at the table with her while dad fixed a breakfast of eggs, bacon, grits, and blueberry muffins. As he did, he gave Peebles, our bird, a play-by-play as he did every morning: "and now you scramble the eggs...whisk, whisk, whisk...and pour them into the pan ..."

Susan noticed something that had - until that moment - escaped our attention: Pebbles wasn't peeping.

Without a word, the four of us mechanically turned our heads toward mom in a slow, deliberate, synchronized motion as she glanced up from the newspaper in horror. All we could hear was the sound of bacon sizzling as we each strained to listen for Pebble's precious peeps...

We realized the unthinkable: Mom had fumigated Pebbles.

Poor Pebbles.

It was a somber day, and I don't think mom ever got over it. We tried to soothe her.

Since it was her birthday, we replaced Pebbles with two other birds - a male and a female; Prince and Princess, but that didn't end well.

Princess killed Prince before the next morning, and from that point on, none of us liked Princess. We thought about letting her fly off into the wild or planting a fake cockroach under her cage for mom to find, but none of us really wanted to go through all of that drama again.

In the end, we gave Princess away. After that, mom only used an all-natural pet-safe roach spray that she made herself. It didn't kill anything - let alone roaches - unless you drowned them, but having that on hand gave mom some peace.

To this day, each time I struggle to recall a fact or remember my own name, my telephone number, or my home address, I think back to my mother doing a series of somersaults down the hallway as she valiantly defended her home from a possible cockroach invasions...and of course, I think about the night Pebbles died...and I think about all of my brain cells that died along with her.

CHAPTER EIGHT

Cousins

As I write this, we're about to celebrate Christmas, and I've been thinking about family a lot lately and especially my cousins - many with children of their own now.

It is so wonderful to see all of us as adults and seeing the next generation being raised in much the same fashion as we were. It is a beautiful thing...but...there are times that I wish we could go back to the Thanksgivings, Christmases, or Fourth of July Celebrations that we shared at Granny/Grandpa's or Grandma/Granddaddy's, or our uncles' or aunts' homes. We always had so much fun.

There is so much for which to be thankful, and there is much to be said about the awe, wonder, mystery, and miracle of the holiday season.

Perhaps one of the greatest miracles of all - at the least with the Miller clan - is that we all survived the many incidental July 4th explosions on Pungo Creek at

Granny and Grandpa's.

I'm sure we were the epitome of the American family that our forefathers envisioned for this great country when they adopted the *Declaration of Independence*: a whole bunch of intoxicated parents hollering directions at us kids as we lit explosives while running up and down on a rickety old dock and bulkhead that had no railing...surrounded by aggressive water moccasins in the pitch black darkness.

The fact that none of us lost a finger or limb or a life is downright astounding.

Happy Holidays, Y'all.

CHAPTER NINE

Grandpa Joe

Born on October 30, 1919, today marks my Grandpa Joe's 99th birthday. He passed away in 2011.

I always enjoyed listening to him talk. He spoke with a gravelly voice and a thick Massachusetts accent. I often find myself impersonating him.

Whenever you'd ask him, "How are you doing?" He'd either reply, "Oh hell, I don't know," or, "Not too bad for an old guy."

Before he died, he asked my dad to contact me and ask me this question: "Would you like your last image of your grandfather to be one where he's upright or one where he's in a box?" If upright, then I needed to see him soon.

During that last visit, the family was sitting around the table making decisions about what would happen when he passed when my aunt asked, "What music do you want at your funeral?" He replied, "Oh hell, I don't know...surprise me!"

My Great-Great-Great Grandfather was Franz

Mueller (1818-1889). After immigrating to America, he changed his name to Francis Miller.

Franz Mueller came from Bavaria. He was a shoemaker by trade. He married an Irish girl. During the Civil War (1861-1865) they relocated their young family to Brunswick, Queens County New Brunswick Canada where he was woodsman, farmer and hunting guide. The farm that they worked has since returned to forest. Franz probably still plied his trade as a shoemaker there since it is listed as his occupation on some census records.

Franz's son, Tom, was instrumental in building St Phillip Roman Catholic Church in Canada and his father, Franz, was the first person buried there.

It isn't clear where Thomas (1848-1914) - my Great-Great Grandfather - was born, but he was buried in New Hampshire.

Thomas's Son, Alfred Fredrick "Fred" Miller (1867-1951) - my Great Grandfather - was born in Brunswick, Canada and died in Barre Plains, Massachusetts.

Fred Miller was born in the rural area of Queens County New Brunswick, Canada. As a child, he lived near his grandparents, the Steens and the Millers. His parents moved to a farm at Head of Millstream in Kings County where the younger siblings were born. There they farmed in spring and summer and harvested timber in the fall and winter. Logs were floated down the Millstream to a mill. Each fall the family would haul barrels to Grand Lake where they would catch fish and salt them for winter food.

Fred left home as a teenager and traveled to the US to

work as a waterboy for the railroad. He eventually became a foreman on the track crew. He took lodging at the Sullivan farm in Barre Plaines where he soon married Margaret Sullivan. In 1905, they lived in Ware and by 1910, they lived on North Brookfield Road, Barre Plaines, before buying a farm on Oakham Road. There, they built a new house in about 1919, leaving the old kitchen attached. In 2015 the place is well cared for by their great-grandson and his family.

At the time of his passing, Joseph Thomas Miller, Sr. - my grandfather - was the last surviving child of Frederick and Margaret's 13 children.

I recently re-read his Obituary where I was reminded of some of his accomplishments. He graduated with a Bachelor of Science Degree in Food Technology and Micro-Biology and a minor in Chemistry from the University of Massachusetts in 1941. Upon graduation, he began a 42-year career in the seafood industry except for the time he served in the Navy during World War II.

He enjoyed Research & Development where he along with fellow food technologists at the Blue Channel Corporation developed the pasteurizing process of crab meat which helped the company become one of the first to can crab meat.

Additionally, he worked to develop recipes for she-crab soup, shrimp bisque, crab cakes as well as deviled crab meat for Harris Atlantic Brand.

After he retired in 1983, he was appointed to various advisory boards for the North Carolina Seafood Industry by Governors James Hunt and James Easley.

* * *

Grandpa married his first love, Claire Elizabeth Tyler, in the summer of 1942. They were married for 55 years before her death in 1997. They had six children. Their youngest, Claire, proceeded both of them in death.

At the time of Grandpa's death, he had 13 grandchildren and 17 great-grandchildren. He also left behind a dear friend, Gladys.

He was an avid duck hunter and became a fantastic golfer after learning the game at age 48. He loved to play bridge and cribbage. He read two newspapers daily, completed crossword puzzles, and tended a garden until months before his passing. Most of all, he was the ultimate Boston Red Sox fan, and almost every year you could hear him utter, "Wait until next year."

Cheers, Grandpa. You were right - you weren't "too bad for an old guy."

CHAPTER TEN

Broken Hip

My paternal grandfather, Joe, was such a fascinating man. He had one of the quickest wits of anyone I've ever known. I am not just saying this because he's my grandfather. He was brilliant in so many ways.

I've often attempted to impersonate his one-liners using his gravelly voice and Massachusetts accent. As I mentioned in the previous chapter, when you'd asked him how he was doing, he always had a quick retort akin to "Hell, I don't know, Michael. Not too bad for an old guy."

After my grandmother died, he had at least two close friends who were women. It feels odd calling them "girlfriends," but you get the idea. I can't recall the name of the first lady, but the second was his longtime sidekick, Ms. Gladys.

He and the first woman had an accident when they were both close to 80-years-old. I don't know if I have all of the details correct, but the story goes something like this:

They'd been out to dinner and were making the drive home when she had to go to the bathroom…right then.

Grandpa pulled over so she could squat beside the car. She lost her balance and fell in a ditch and was unable to get out so my grandfather had to pull her out. He said that it was like lifting a sack of "badadoes" (potatoes in Massachusetts speak).

At the hospital, they learned that she had broken a hip.

A few days later, my Grandfather was at some event - maybe the Rotary Club - and the woman's son was also there. Someone joked with her son, "I heard Joe was getting lucky with your mom and broke her hip."
Without missing a beat, my grandfather commented, "Hell, if I were getting lucky, I would've broken both her hips."

Good ol' Joe.

PART TWO

Don't Make Fun of Me

CHAPTER ELEVEN

Don't Know Much

For the record, if you ever have a question about history, I'm not the one to ask. I just make music and try to write funny stories. Besides, I nearly failed American History...twice; once in high school and again in college.

I was so dumb in college that I took History as a "condensed" summer school course thinking that "condensed" meant "less work." Nope. It meant that I had to do three months of work in 2.5 weeks.

The professor looked so old, white, and dusty as he stood outside the door on the first day of class that I mistook him for a statue. He was the spitting image of Colonel Sanders, but he later told us that people always thought he looked like Kenny Rogers - which he took as a supreme compliment.

He had a wealth of knowledge. I presume he knew so much about American History because he had lived through most of it.

I wrote 87-and-a-half papers for that course. Back

then, all of my work was handwritten. Midway through my 88th paper, the tip of my index finger rotted off. All I could do was write, "It is Finished!" in blood, and then I breathed a sigh of relief.

As I turned in that paper, I told the professor that I knew I had failed - the paper and the course.

Knowing that I was a music major, he offered to give me extra credit if I could sing a song - right there on the spot - but it had to be a song summarizing the most important thing I had learned about history during his class.

Without missing a beat and with a twinkle in my eye, I sang the rousing chorus of Kenny Roger's *The Gambler*.

By the grace of God and the immortal words of Kenny Rogers, I passed that class with a C-minus.

In truth, everything I know about History I learned from Ken Burns. He knows how to turn a monologue about cooking cornbread over an open flame with frostbitten hands in a snowdrift 9-feet high sound like something you might want to try someday.

I am a little embarrassed to admit this, but I fell asleep during the last episode of his Civil War documentary and missed how the war was won. I didn't feel so bad after watching an episode of Discovery Channel's *Moonshiners* where one of the toothless Shiners said something like 'we's been fighting the onion ever since my great-grand-pappy was a youngin.' I'm sure he meant "Union," and I am fairly certain he's unaware that the war is, in fact, over.

Needless to say, I have a great appreciation for those who know a lot about history.

CHAPTER TWELVE

Visiting Churches

While attending church is not a priority for all college students, it was for me. I thought I was going to be a pastor until I saw the light.

During my freshman and sophomore years of college, I used Sunday mornings as opportunities to attend a number of churches; different sizes and denominations.

One Sunday morning, in particular, stands out.

I was excited about what I would experience as I drove to one of the largest churches in the area.

When I pulled into the parking lot, it was so large that I questioned whether or not I had mistakenly driven to *Carowinds* amusement park. Fortunately, the driver of an extended - or stretched - golf cart reassured me that I was in the right place when he offered to shuttle me up to the enormous doors of the proportionally enormous church building.

A greeter held the door open for me. Upon seeing him, I felt under-dressed. I only had one tie and one jacket with me at college. They were inexpensive and they looked, felt, and fit that way compared to the fine clothes worn by the men and women who were making their way down the long hallway to the Sanctuary.

There were *a lot* of folks there and even though I was still quite a distance away from the sanctuary, I could hear the murmur of the large congregation inside.

I passed a few church offices, a nursery, a parlor, a library, the Sacristy, and the restrooms (I should have gone to the restroom while I had the chance).

I said hello to an usher. He looked like he worked for the Secret Service and instead of replying back, he assertively handed me a bulletin. He did not smile at all and seemed to give me a once-over to determine whether or not I was dressed well enough to enter the sanctuary. Fortunately, he let me in.

To say that the inside of this place was beautiful would be an understatement. It was breath-taking with a soaring cathedral ceiling, stained glass windows throughout, and there were organ pipes covering nearly every inch of the front wall behind the choir loft and pulpit.

I went down the far-left aisle between the pews and the exterior wall. I walked all the way to the front but couldn't find a place to sit. Yes, there were open spots but no one was really interested in inviting me to sit. Instead, it seemed like people were intentionally busying themselves in order to avoid eye contact with me. They seemed like a bunch of squatters staking claim over their pew.

As I stood at the front of the church looking for a place to sit, a hush fell over the crowd. I turned toward the front of the church to see a choir wearing white robes filling the choir loft. There must have been 100 of them. They found their place and remained standing until the choir director signaled for them to sit all at once. When they did, you could almost feel a rush of wind in the room.

There were some empty pews in the balcony so I began making my way upstairs while trying my best not to draw any attention to myself. I tried to be discreet as I climbed the stairs but no matter how lightly I stepped, those polished terrazzo floors were so squeaky clean that, with every step, the soles of my shoes sent an echo bouncing around the stairwell that sounded like, and was nearly as loud as, a fire alarm. With the congregation so eerily quiet, I felt like all eyes - and ears - were on me.

Fortunately, the silence in the room was broken by a church bell in the steeple chiming the hour followed immediately by a lush organ prelude.

I finally found a place where I sat and listened with my hands folded across my lap and my eyes closed while the organist played for about 3 minutes. Though soft, the music filled the room and I felt like I was being wrapped in a warm, plush blanket.

As the end of the prelude neared, the intensity built and I readied my hands to clap in response. The organist held her last chord for several seconds and I clapped...once...one clap...only one...because *no one else clapped*. Not wanting to be blamed, I acted like it wasn't me by glancing at the people sitting behind me with the same look of disgust I saw on the faces of the people who were giving me the stink-eye...in the name of the Lord, of course.

As the organ launched into the introduction of the first hymn, everyone stood. As I picked up my bulletin to see what was going on, about fifteen half-sheets of paper - all different colors - fell out and down below the pew in front of me. Because each row was higher than the next, I could not reach below the pew to get the paper.

Everyone was singing before I stood back up. I quickly opened the bulletin to find the hymn number and kept repeating to myself, "174, 174, 174, 174," until I could find the page.

In the rack attached to the pew in front of me was a blue book, a grey book, and a black book. I figured that the black book would be the Bible…and it was. The blue book had hymns but the first hymn number was number 250; that's so confusing.

After fumbling through the grey book, I found the hymn just as they were finishing the second verse. When the third verse started, I noticed that they weren't singing the song I was looking at, so I looked in the bulletin again. Yep, hymn 174. Then, I looked at the hymnal I was holding and saw that I had turned to *147* instead.

By the time I got to the right page, they were singing the final word of the hymn, but at least I was able to join in on the "Amen" (which wasn't even printed in the music).

It was only then that I noticed five of the U.S. Supreme Court Justices enter the sanctuary. That all sat down at the same time on chairs that looked like royal thrones facing the congregation. It almost looked like they were waiting to hear testimony.

One of them stood up and approached the pulpit. It wasn't a judge or a college president, it was an associate minister. I had never attended a church where pastors wore well-starched black academic robes - how fancy.

The microphone was off when he began to speak so he tapped it until the sound man turned him up. I am sure that whatever he said was massively important but all I could hear was Ben Stein's voice in *Ferris Bueller's Day Off*... "Bueller, Bueller, Bueller." He had about as much enthusiasm and charisma as a piece of used sand paper. If younger readers don't know of Ben Stein, just imagine an *unenthusiastic* version Mitch McConnell.

According to the bulletin, he was giving announcements concerning the *Life of the Church*. If his affect represented "the life of the church," then someone should have called a mortician. By the time he finished, I believe that he'd read all of the announcements verbatim from the fifteen sheets of colored paper that fell out of my bulletin earlier.

As he left the pulpit, a choir of 25 elementary school kids walked in single file to the front of the church where their director placed them in their appropriate places on the stairs; which took seven-and-a-half minutes.

Once they were standing still, the director backed away a few feet to see how they looked. Apparently, not everyone was *exactly* where she wanted them. She then began to signal to certain singers - who really didn't know who she was pointing at - to move a *millimeter* to the right or to the left. The director took this process as seriously as she would docking an aircraft carrier, but the kids were so confused that all of them moved side-to-side in an effort to appease her. When she realized that her efforts were fruitless, she gave up and nodded to the pianist to start playing.

Even though the song was slow and soft, the director seemed to conduct hard, fast, erratically, and with as much drama as Leonard Bernstein did conducting the *1812 Overture*. It was just *too* much.

The kids were hard to hear at first. As they ended the first verse, you could hear the director whisper very loudly and with precise annunciation, "Sing Louder." She demanded more volume at the end of every line… so much so that I began to think that "sing louder" was part of the song. By the end of the song, they were screaming as loud as their little lungs would let them.

As they yelled the final note - which seemed to go on about 20 seconds longer than anything acceptable - a couple of the singers passed out from sheer exhaustion, and I think I noticed a trace of blood on the chins of a few of those little cherubs.

I could tell by the smiles in the room that everyone thought this was cute. The congregation broke into thunderous applause as the ushers carried the weaker kids out on stretchers. This was the only time anyone clapped during the service - except for my solitary clap after the magnificent prelude.

Several years later, I learned that formal congregations only clap after children sing, a moving testimony in which someone was "saved," or when it is announced that the church has ended the budget year in the black.

During the sermon, the preacher read the scriptures in such a way that the story came to life. I was riveted by his interpretation of the text and his delivery.

Others seemed far less interested...a few men in the choir and at least one of the associate pastors looked as though they might have lost consciousness...or maybe they were simply slain in the spirit.

I almost broke the clapping rule again when he finished because the message was so good but there was no time. A split-second after he concluded his sermon, the organist launched into another hymn. I had the hymnal ready and joined my voice with the robust sound of the congregation.

After that, *another* pastor stepped up to the pulpit and asked, "Christian, what do you believe?"

I thought it was a rhetorical question but the congregation started chanting something...and it was not the *Lord's Prayer* which I knew by heart...two versions of it.

I later learned that it was the *Athanasian Creed*. It was one of the most boring things I've ever come across... including the brief period in my life when I read VCR and DVD manuals to help me go to sleep.

The text for this *Statement of Belief* was apparently printed on one of the colorful sheets of paper I dropped beneath the pew earlier.

I stood there in silence with my eyes closed and shaking my head in affirmation for the entire fifteen minutes hoping that if anyone saw me they'd think that I was having a profound moment instead of thinking I was a heathen.

Then, we entered into my *favorite* part of the service: the "Time of Welcome." Another robed man standing on the podium asked, "Do we have any first-time visitors?"

Everyone in the balcony looked around eagerly and, one by one, their eyes locked on me. They seemed to stare at me as if they were a group of Hyenas circling up for a kill.

Visitors were asked to stand, and I did…reluctantly. An usher put an embroidered rose sticker on the lapel of my shirt like it was a ceremonial rite of passage. The pastor then invited everyone to greet one another.

One of the people who met me was a high-spirited older woman who was the type that might pinch my tush had I turned around…you know the type: old looking but very young at heart…who acts as a provocateur with her rebellious ways…like going to Denny's after dark.

After her polite welcome, she asked me if I was married or had kids. She laughed at my attempt at humor when I answered, "Not that I know of."

I was somewhat expecting her to slip me her phone number on the way out but that did not happen.

This *Time of Welcome* felt excruciatingly long. I just wanted the service to end because by this point, my bladder felt like it was going to burst.

Next was the offering during which the choir sang.

When the anthem finally ended, everyone stood without a cue and sang *The Doxology* from memory. I did not know the words. I am sure that they were printed on one of 15 pages of the bulletin that had fallen under the pew, so I made up the words.

MY words might not have been right, but I sang it with strength and conviction.

"Praise God from humans blessings grow.
Praise him and preachers here I know.
Praise him above the heaven's boast.
Praise father's son who's whole and most."
…or something like that.

In the closing prayer, it was so quiet you could hear my stomach growling throughout the whole church. I just wanted the service to be over so that I could scurry off to the restroom and then grab something to eat on the way home. I was starving.

The final hymn began and this time I was on the right page and really enjoyed singing with all those people and that powerful pipe organ.

Apparently, I missed the note that verse 3 was to be omitted. I was halfway through the third verse before I noticed a middle-aged woman glaring at me as if I had stolen her purse or slapped her child. I figured out my mistake and made it to the finish line for the fourth verse with the rest of the crowd. All too happy it was over, I sang "Amen" as loudly as I could.

I put the books back in the rack, grabbed my bulletin, and started to leave. I could not get out of there fast enough!!!! Has your bladder ever been so full that you had chills?

Everyone was sitting back down. *WHY?*

I thought about making a run for it but before I could, a loud noise that reminded me of bagpipes starting up nearly ruptured my eardrums.

I looked up and saw dust billowing and belching out of organ pipes - pipes that had not been used in years apparently. I was forced back down into my seat by the volume of chords played by the Organist.

I tried to fight it and internally began singing, "Stand up! Stand Up for Jesus," but was overthrown and sat back down. Actually, it was more like I had been pinned back down...held against my will to the hard pew by the sheer and unruly power of that organ. The Organist had unleashed a sonic kryptonite rendering all in ear-shot powerless until she released her final note.

As the last of the organ's sound echoed off the back way wall, I started clapping and shouting "Hallelujah!!"...not because the music moved me...but because I was finally free to move.

Sure, the postlude might have transported some people to "Glory land" but I nearly wet my pants so I ran out the door in fear that the organist might start another song.

70

CHAPTER THIRTEEN

Sports

This might come as a surprise, but I am not an athlete. I mean, I can walk all day long - faster than most people - only because I have the thighs of a bull, but give me a basketball and you'll spend the rest of your long life watching me try my best to score a field goal.

When I played soccer and baseball as a kid I was always positioned in the least important roles; just call me "water boy."

I was one heck of a bowler, though.

Oh yeah…and badminton; give me a racket and one of those whatchamacallits and I'll hit at least 8 out of every 10 over the net - which for me is pretty good.

Still, I was at the baseball fields all the time. I worked in the concession stand and kept score.

For a while, though, I was a Crossing Guard to help people cross a road to get to some auxiliary fields.

One day, while working the street, I thought I was having a cardiac episode and nearly quit my job, but it turned out that it was just a chili dog that didn't agree with me.

Another time, I was wearing my orange vest and holding my 25 lb. wooden Stop Sign when the driver of a truck - who was paying more attention to his son putting on cleats than driving - almost ran over me.

He actually did make contact, but thank goodness for my powerful thighs.

Somehow I avoided injury by hurling my body across the two-lane road and into a ditch where I did a tuck-and-roll maneuver. I guess that watching all of those episodes of the *Six Million Dollar Man* really paid off.

When I look back at those days, I only have one thought: thank goodness for music.

CHAPTER FOURTEEN

I was Spanked

I was spanked...not recently...but a spanking was a potential consequence for any list of things my parents deemed inappropriate when I was a kid.

Many such offenses were well established, but some could be added to the list instantly and without a perceivable warning. Yes, what "crossed the line" could be a guessing game at times, but it rarely took more than a split second to know whether or not I'd crossed it.

Parents have the difficult task of discovering what works best with each child.

We three Miller kids each responded differently. For me, my parents used "shock and awe" techniques: quick and swift movements of the hand with a trajectory that I could only determine a moment after impact.

For my brother, all my mother had to do was give "the look," and he'd melt.

My sister required my parents to be relatively fit because she'd run...fast. Susan was more agile, but mom and dad had more stamina. Susan's goal was to find a place where they couldn't reach.

For some children, all it takes is Time-out. That wouldn't have worked for me, I don't think.

For some, it is the dreaded wooden spoon. A mother need only display the very end of the handle from the pocket of her purse to deter inappropriateness. That's enough to remind the child of what happens when the full spoon is hastily yanked out at Walmart — effectively silencing a tantrum over not getting twenty-five cents to put in the chewing gum machine.

In our home, there was always a lingering threat of the fly-swatter. In the hands of my mother, that was a deadly weapon - and not just for flies.

I don't have any kids that I'm aware of, but believing in miracles, I know that anything could happen. If the Virgin Mary could have a kid, it could happen to me, but it would require another immaculate conception. Fortunately, I've not had an encounter with an Angelic OBGYN.

I only know the pressures parents face by reflection on my own childhood and by observation...very close and extremely judgmental observation.

In my family, we were not allowed to cuss nor were we allowed to say a whole dictionary of words including "shut-up" and "stupid."

We always had to say "Yes, ma'am," "No, ma'am," "Yes, sir," and, "No, sir."

We always had to ask permission to be excused from the dinner table - to throw something away, to clear our plates, or to run to the bathroom.

We had to call every adult by their appropriate titles: Doctor, Pastor, Mr., Mrs., or Ms...and first name - unless they were teachers or doctors - in which case we used their last name.

I lived near two of my teachers, and to this day I still can't use first names for Mrs. Esarey or Mrs. Mackenzie. As an adult, they've both asked that I call them by their first names, but that is utterly impossible for me.

My mom always called my dad's dad "Mr. Miller," and my dad always called my mom's mom "Mrs. Fletcher."

I was a bit shocked when I first attended the University of Washington where, for the first time, I heard students calling professors by first names - to their faces - in class, no less.

At Winthrop, there were one or two professors whose first names would be used outside of class; Don Rogers, for instance. His first and last names went well together...it was right...and appropriate. In person, however, no student would dare call him Don - not even students who were the same age or older than he...and no one would refer to Dr. Edgerton (Dr. E., for short) as Bob inside or outside of class unless they were trying to be funny.

To be clear, what I witnessed - students calling professors by their first names - was NOT a sign of disrespect. It was just the cultural norm - and that's perfectly fine.

I personally enjoy the formality of using titles for others. In a school setting, I like the boundary such titles impose between teachers and students - but that's just me.

I know high school teachers who are able to maintain an authoritative role still while having students call them by their first names. When I taught high school, my students began calling me "Miller." That was fine because I always felt that "Mr. Miller" was my grandpa.

When it came to respecting my parents - or disrespecting them - I learned that if you're going to do something terrible or say nasty around my mother, you'd better be at least an arm's length away. I recall drying dishes while she washed and apparently I was too close. I don't know what I said, but before I knew exactly what happened, I found myself staggering across the kitchen with a soapy hand-print across my cheek.

Church seemed to be the place that caused the most anxiety for my mother - no, not the church itself... taking her kids to church and expecting them to behave. So, she'd split us up; me, Mom, Susan, Dad, and Tim.

While that was the best approach, it didn't always work. It seemed that my siblings and I could psychically misbehave with one another - all three of us simultaneously acting up.

Mom would lovingly put her arm over my shoulder, hug me while pulling me in closer for what appeared to be a warm and loving mother-son moment.

Without anyone else in the room aware, she'd use the speed, accuracy, and intensity of a ninja and pop the side of my cheek so swiftly that it almost seemed to me that the power in the building flickered for less than a split second.

She'd then make eye contact with me with what appeared to onlookers to be a smile, but the look in her eyes and the words I was forced to lip-read were anything but pleasant.

If that did not yield her desired outcome, her left hand would find its way to my left leg. While still holding me close - which felt more like a Boa Constrictor than a loving embrace - she'd squeeze the muscle in my thigh so hard my eyes would water.

Amazingly, she could do all of this while still paying attention to the sermon, innocently glancing around the sanctuary, and occasionally exchanging a friendly smile with another church member - and no one except the two of us really knew what was going on: I was being forced into submission against my will. There was no use resisting. She had won.

To add insult to injury, as she released her death-grip on my leg, she'd feign innocence and whisper, "You almost made me hurt my hand."

These physical responses didn't teach me that hitting was ok. It didn't teach me to handle my problems with violence. It taught me that there were real consequences for my actions.

While we were never physically beaten or abused, I think that we three Miller kids would testify in a court of law that mom's "look of disappointment" - which was swifter than any wooden spoon - was a form of emotional abuse (that's intended to be funny). I'd rather have 15 spankings than see that look once.

I don't really remember the spankings or what caused them, but her "look" occasionally flashes across the screen of my mind's eye, and I feel a bitter sense of regret for whatever I did that warranted receiving it in the first place.

Thank goodness for the unconditional love of parents. I sure needed it. If I'm honest, I still need it...but don't we all?

PART THREE

Mom

CHAPTER FIFTEEN

Let There Be Peace on Earth

Let there be peace on earth, and let it begin with me.

In 1997, as I was preparing for my first Christmas concert as a public high school music educator, my mother who had just been diagnosed with terminal cancer wanted to know what my students were going to sing.

It didn't seem that she'd be well enough to make the trip to attend my first concert so I went through the song list for her.

She then asked, "What about *Let There Be Peace on Earth?*"

"What about it?," I asked.

"Well, it isn't Christmas without that song."

She sang that song around our house every time there seemed to be strife in our family unit...therefore, I heard it often.

She made a deal with me that she'd attend all of the concerts in which I programmed the song - for as long as she could - so I programed it on *every* concert - Christmas and Spring.

She died four years later, but she made the nearly 6-hour round-trip for every concert regardless of her health.

A few weeks after her passing, my undergraduate choral conducting mentor, Dr. Robert Edgerton, invited me to come to his house. When I arrived, he handed me a hand-written manuscript of his new arrangement of *Let there be peace on earth*. In memory of her, he dedicated that arrangement to the Lancaster Chamber Choir, a community choir I directed at the time.

He continued to tweak his arrangement and it evolved and expanded into the version that is now published. I've since written my own setting, too.

The song, *Let There Be Peace on Earth*, takes me to a special place - it takes me home, it reminds me of my mother, and it reminds me that we are all brothers and sisters and should all strive to live in harmony.

CHAPTER SIXTEEN

Miracle on King Street

About 15 years ago I began writing a book about some interesting life experiences in order to preserve them. Several of those stories involved my family and some of the bizarre happenings surrounding my mother's passing.

I called the book, *You're Not Going to Believe This.* I decided to call the second book, *You're Not Going to Believe This, Either.*

I never finished the project because the stories felt too personal to share publicly, and I preferred telling the stories in person. My writing might not do justice to the stories, but I hope to share with you a glimpse of divinity.

It was Tuesday, August 7, 2001. I received a call from my sister, Susan, that Mom was in the hospital and the situation was dire.

I made my way to Roper Hospital in Charleston, South Carolina, where, along with my family, I spent much of Wednesday and Thursday.

On Friday morning, I sat alone with Mom as she slept

uneasily. In silence, I contemplated the reality of the situation.

Mom had lived far beyond the life expectancy for her type and stage of cancer. She wanted to live long enough to see my brother get married. One month earlier, we celebrated Tim and Nicole's wedding.

At their reception, Mom partied more than anyone else...and she gave one doozie of a toast.

In hindsight, we should have told the D.J. not to give her a microphone, but I am sure that she would have found a way to give her impromptu toast anyway.

She had a lot to say. Perhaps the most poignant moment came as she fought back tears and proclaimed, "We are so lucky to *finally* have a daughter."

This, of course, did not sit well with my sister, Susan. Fortunately, Susan saw the humor and *loves* to tell the story.

Mom was feeling no pain and was having so much fun that she took the party back to our house. That night, there was no indication that her health would significantly decline just days after the wedding.

When Dad, Susan, Tim, and Nicole arrived at the hospital that Friday afternoon, Susan held an envelope of wedding pictures taken by our aunt that had come in the mail. I remember thumbing through photos but not really looking at them...I was too numb...I needed a break...and some fresh air...so I went for a walk.

As I strolled along King Street, out of nowhere it began to rain – not mist, not sprinkle – **RAIN!** You haven't lived until you've experienced a thunderstorm in Charleston.

Within mere seconds, I was nearly soaked...so I ran into the closest store – the *Daughters of St. Paul Catholic Bookstore.*

After browsing around, I ended up in the music section where I began listening to some recordings. There were no other customers in the store; it was just me and the nuns.

About ten minutes later, I heard the door open and was surprised to see Tim and Nicole.

The three of us were making small talk when Tim and Nicole recognized a nun they had met before.

After some pleasantries, she said, "I've been praying for your mom. How is Patricia doing?"

...Awkward...

Our mom's name is Donna.

She chuckled at her mistake, "I've been praying for Patricia all along...but God knows who I meant...

...We must pray for Donna...now!"

She led us to a small chapel in the back of the store.

As we crossed the threshold into the chapel, we felt compelled to kneel. It was as though we had entered God's Throne Room.

She began to pray. She hadn't spoken five words before the three of us were crying. It was the single-most touching and sincere prayer I've ever heard.

She concluded her prayer,

"...God, we ask that you bring healing to Patricia...*Oh, God*...Donna...*Jesus!* AMEN."

Our tears gave way to laughter. We needed that

prayer and that laughter more than anything else in the world in that moment.

Then, she asked us to wait there while she went upstairs.

When she returned, she had 4 small icon pendants that had been blessed by Pope John Paul II. She explained their individual significance as she gave one to each of us. Lastly, she gave us an icon of "Jesus – The All-Powerful" that she wanted Mom to have. She instructed us to tell Mom that, "Healing was on the way."

We hurried back to the hospital and were surprised to find Mom alert and talking.

It was a *miracle*!!! It is hard to explain the drastic change in the way she looked, acted, and felt, but truly, it defied explanation.

We gave Mom the icon and the nun's message as we each shared an account of our experience. Then, we each took turns looking at the wedding pictures.

One picture stood out. It was of Mom and her cousin, Helen, standing together in front of a glass wall in the back of the church after the wedding.

I think it was Susan who saw it first…no one else had noticed the reflection above mom in the glass. It was an image of Jesus cast from a beautiful stained-glass window at the front of the church. The image somewhat bore a resemblance to the image of the "Jesus – The All-Powerful" icon.

Chills ran up and down my spine when I first saw the image of Jesus above mom in the photo. The picture still has the same effect on me.

* * *

Unbeknownst to us, the Catholic Priest affiliated with the bookstore was at the hospital visiting and praying for Mom at the same time we were in the store.

To everyone's amazement, Mom went home the next day.

The image of Jesus seeming to float above my mother reminds me of a quote:
"If you knew who walked beside you at all times along your path, you could never experience fear or doubt again."

CHAPTER SEVENTEEN

Beyond the Classroom...Beyond Explanation

It was Friday, September 28, 2001. Mom had been in the hospital for weeks but this day was different as she began drifting in and out of consciousness.

At some point that morning, I said to her, "Do not go gentle into that good night...Rage, rage against the dying of the light." This poem by Dylan Thomas was assigned reading in my twelfth-grade British Literature class taught by Mrs. Kay Metzger-Merkel.

I can still remember the first day of her class. She calmly walked in, sat on a stool, called roll, and then asked us to take out pencils and paper for our very first test.

Using the book, *Cultural Literacy: What Every American Needs to Know*, she called out a series of topics; words, celebrities, athletes, movie titles, and lyrics to songs, among other things. We were to write a brief description about each of these items that we − as culturally literate Americans − should know something about.

At the conclusion of this exercise, my paper was still

blank. Thankfully, that assignment was not graded.

'I am *not* here to teach British Literature,

...*nor* am I here to teach you how to write.'

When she wanted to make a point, she could have given Alan Rickman a run for his money when it comes to articulating words slowly and pointedly with crisp, percussive consonants to emphasize their shared use of sardonic humor (Rickman is the reason *Professor Snape* my favorite *Harry Potter* character).

'I am here...to prepare *you*...for life (strong f)...

...and based on how little you know about these subjects...

I have a lot (strong t)

...of work (strong k)

...to do...(strong t and d)'

Everyone at Stratford High School knew her reputation of being extremely strict, and she was, but she was also an extremely effective teacher.

I thrive under teachers who expect much from me. Four years after high school, I aced British Literature in college without hardly cracking a book thanks to her. In retrospect, I wish that she had been my math teacher, too.

In the hospital that day, I recognized that she had also taught my brother and Susan. I knew that that was the case before, but it didn't seem meaningful until that moment. It then occurred to me that she was the *only* teacher at that school who taught all three of us.

This was not news to Dad. At the beginning of Susan's senior year (1995–1996), Dad attended Open

House where he met each of her teachers. He joked with Mrs. Merkel that she had been the only teacher fortunate enough to teach *all three* of his children.

She responded directly, "No, sir. You are mistaken...

They are the fortunate ones." She was not joking.

Because our mother was a teacher, and because we knew so many teachers, we knew that Mrs. Merkel's role as a strict taskmaster was just a facade. She was very kind and loving.

Her name echoed in mom's hospital room throughout the day as we shared stories about our time in her class.

Susan told the story of how, for Christmas, they decorated Mrs. Merkel with Christmas lights and paraded her up and down the hall in a rolling desk chair singing carols.

The humor of this event might be lost on you because you do not know her. Suffice it to say that allowing students to do this was highly out of character...and making noise in the hallways of Stratford High School during class time was enough to warrant death by firing squad if the principal found out.

There might have only been one other occasion in which she was not in complete command of her students. A few months later, Mrs. Merkel announced that she was about to turn 70 and wanted to have a party. Susan and her classmates made it happen and, once again, they were raucous...but hey, you only turn 70 once.

That evening, we left Mom sleeping and returned to

our home in Goose Creek for a short time before going to dinner at our favorite local restaurant, *Los Arcos*.

Moments before we left, the doorbell rang.

Dad opened the door and looked stunned. His voice seemed to quiver a bit, "Look who it is...come on in..."

It was Mrs. Merkel.

No Joke!

She had *NEVER* been to our house before that night!

Seeing her standing there made each of us cry... including my dad. It was hard to explain to her why her presence made us all so emotional.

At that time, she was still teaching at 75 and was as sharp and demanding as ever.

She told us that we had been on her mind all day, and she felt compelled to do something for us.

After collecting money from other teachers, many of whom taught us, she purchased a stockpile of food so that we would have one less thing to worry about in the days ahead.

"You need your strength, and you need to eat," she said.

She was right. Little did we know that we would wake to a call in the middle of the night summoning us to the hospital; a ritual that would be required of us every night until... until it was no longer necessary.

As we unloaded the groceries from her car, she explained that she would not be at Mom's funeral – whenever it was – because she simply did not like funerals.

* * *

After the funeral eight days later, many of Mom's friends provided lunch in the Fellowship Hall at the church for all in attendance.

I get choked up when I recall how some of the very people who taught us in school were there honoring mom and supporting our family by cooking and serving the meal, as well as cleaning up. Mrs. Merkel was there, too, collecting and washing dishes.

Before returning to my home in Rock Hill after mom's service, I shared a cup of tea with Mrs. Merkel in her living room as we talked about life and death. She was all too familiar with the grief and pain that comes with losing loved ones.

She gave me a framed work of art created by her sister – a gifted artist who died tragically many years before.

The Memory Store is a rectangular collage featuring rows and rows of doors and doorways; all different shapes and sizes. There are doorways within doorways. Some doors open inward and others outward, and in each doorway is a person who appears to walk either toward you or away from you. Its overall hue is reddish – presumably suggesting the color of blood – and the entire piece is slightly out of focus.

I think the piece depicts our blurred perception of souls entering and departing our world.

I am still in contact with Mrs. Merkel even though she has moved to Florida to be closer to family and it brings me great joy to know that she has read this story. She also knows the profound impact she has had on my life and that of my family.

Michael Austin Miller

CHAPTER EIGHTEEN

Get My Shoes. I'm Goin' Home

"I have to get my shoes, get the baby, and go home."

I can't tell you how many times we heard Mom say those haunting words as she drifted in and out of consciousness during the last days of her life. By then, cancer had all but destroyed her body. She was barely hanging on but was doing all she could to cling to life.

It was a difficult time and not just for us. Across our country, people were dealing with grief after the 9-11 attacks as my mother's health began its rapid decline.

Like so many who die of a terminal illness, she had a sudden and drastic improvement as family members gathered in her hospital room the Saturday before she passed. As we watched the Clemson vs. Georgia Tech football game, she was surprisingly alert, communicative, and in good spirits, but after everyone left, we realized that we had just experienced the beginning of the end.

I had to leave that night in order to play the piano for a church service the next morning. I wrestled over being three hours away from my family, but I knew one thing:

Mom would want me to honor my commitments. I also knew that if I was supposed to be by her side when she took her last breath, I would be.

Before sunrise the next morning, I received a call from my sister, Susan, who shared that Mom was dying. As it is often said, "the darkest hour is just before dawn," and that was true for Mom. That was Sunday and for the next four mornings we repeated that pattern and for the next four mornings her Oncologist, Dr. David Ellison, was surprised to see we were still there.

This prolonged dying process was very hard to witness but as the doctor reminded us each morning, Mom had surpassed his expectations at every turn along her journey. He even went as far as declaring her treatment a "success" - not because she had beaten cancer, but because she had lived so long and with a relatively good quality of life.

In those last days, she was sleeping much deeper than normal.

She was tired; tired of treatment, tired of fighting, tired of the medications, tired of being in the bed, tired of the pain, and tired of grieving.

Not only had she been grieving the loss of her own life and losing her connection with those she would leave behind, she felt our grief, too. She felt our pain as we struggled to navigate this journey with her. She felt our pain as we absorbed the reality that she'd soon be gone and we'd eventually leave the hospital one last time — without her.

As her body began growing tired of breathing, the full weight of this experience hit me and I knew that all too soon she'd stop breathing.

"I have to get my shoes, get the baby, and go home."

I tried to decipher what she meant:
"Get my shoes." She must mean "get ready."
"Get the baby." She must be referring to herself.
"Go home" clearly mean Heaven.

When you're watching a loved one dying, you grasp at any form of hope. Perhaps that's what I was doing… trying to feel a sense of hope while desperately wishing things were different…hoping things would turn around…hoping we'd be able to go home - as a whole family - and return to life as normal.

"I have to get my shoes, get the baby, and go home."

Trying to make sense of this refrain was useless, really, because she wasn't thinking clearly…or was she?

One night, my brother and I were a little spooked when she asked us the names of the people standing behind us, but to our knowledge no one was there.

That wasn't the only time she reported seeing beings we couldn't perceive. She mentioned her brother's name a few times, and I wouldn't doubt that she had some visitors from the other side. I am also inclined to believe that, if anyone was going to see beings from the other side, it would have been her.

We were all in denial - which is to be expected, I guess - and it played out in a variety of ways. For me, one obvious sign was my inability to say the word "hospital." I kid you not - each time I meant to say "hospital," the word "hotel" came out. It was as though the word didn't even exist in my vocabulary.

Each time mom talked about getting her shoes, the baby, and going home, she seemed to grow more determined. Her concern for the "baby," in particular, became obvious, but we could never get her to tell us what she meant.

That refrain began to come less often as she began to fade, but it was one of the last things we ever heard her say.

"I have to get my shoes, get the baby, and go home."

On Wednesday - the day before she passed - our family decided to limit who came into the room because we knew that she wouldn't want people seeing her in that condition. We also knew that she certainly wouldn't want people remembering her in that state.

My father, sister, and I were in her hospital room when her cousin, his wife, and their daughter, Jennifer, came to see mom for the last time.

Because he was in the military, we had seen them very little over the years but were glad they came to say goodbye. They were her very last visitors.

Tears were shed - which wasn't unexpected - but Jennifer, who was around my age, was really weeping; especially as she leaned down to hug mom and whisper her farewell.

Susan and I then went into the hallway with Jennifer who grew even more emotional. Of the three of us, she seemed to be having the hardest time.

In truth, we Miller kids had mastered the art of putting on a brave face when others were around - as long as no one touched us. Anytime someone would ask Susan, Tim, Nicole (Tim's wife), or me how we were doing, we'd jokingly say, "I'm Fine...just don't touch me." We were kind of serious though because even a light hug or soft pat on the back could start an avalanche of tears.

In response to Jennifer's sorrow, Susan and I felt compelled to tell her that we knew mom would be ok and that we were going to be ok.

As Jennifer collected herself, she said, "I know...but I just had a miscarriage and lost a baby."

The baby!

With a sense of urgency, Susan and I said "the baby" at the exact same time.

The feeling of shock we had in that moment was something I had never felt before and haven't felt since.

Chills ran throughout my entire body as every hair stood on end and tears welled up in my eyes. I could even feel my insides shaking. Susan had the same sensations as we hurriedly told Jennifer how mom had repeatedly uttered the words. "I have to get my shoes, get the baby, and go home."

Jennifer's voice trembled as she told us what she had just whispered into mom's ear: "Please watch over my baby."

Michael Austin Miller

CHAPTER NINETEEN

The LePines

This story is not only mine to tell as it involved two others who have read this already and who helped me give an accurate account. Thank you, Glenn and PJ.

In February 1982, my family moved to Cherry Hill – a new subdivision in Goose Creek, SC. In addition to moving into a new home, my family found itself surrounded by people who would eventually become more like family than just neighbors.

Glenn and Paulette (PJ) LePine were among the first neighbors we met.

One Saturday morning, I slammed my fingers in a car door; an older car that was built like a tank and with doors so heavy they might as well have been armor-plated.

Knowing that Mr. LePine's work involved splinting and casting in an orthopedic office and PJ was an OR Registered Nurse, my mother rushed me to their home. There was no significant damage, but Mr. LePine put a splint on my fingers and recommended I see a doctor.

The LePine family quickly became very dear friends of ours, and Mr. and Mrs. LePine would later play a significant role in my mother's final hours.

I felt broken, empty, and lost as I sat alone with mom in the hospital two days before she passed away. Whether she knew I was present that morning or not didn't matter.

As much as I hated the situation, I desperately wanted to freeze that moment in time because I knew that there weren't many more moments left.

I was playing a CD compilation of all the music that would be used at mom's "Celebration of Life." Sara Grove's soothing song, *What Do I Know?* was floating softly on the air when there was a knock at the door.

I was beyond surprised to see Glenn and PJ. This visit was met with mixed emotions as it would be the last time they'd see my mother, but we each felt an overwhelming sense of gratitude for Glenn's life.

Mrs. LePine is easily one of the kindest people I've ever known, but if I am honest, I was a little scared of Mr. LePine when I was a kid. In addition to being tall and broad, he had a larger-than-life personality with the gift of gab and a dry, smart, and quick wit.

Perhaps it was his line of work, but he usually appeared – at least to a younger me - to be very serious and matter-of-fact. There was a sternness about him, and it would be hard to imagine him being easily moved to tears.

The LePines were members of Immaculate Conception Catholic Church (the same church where my brother and his wife were married a few months before mom passed), but I couldn't have imagined that one day I'd find myself talking so intimately about God with Mr. LePine.

Things were very different that morning, however, as life for the LePines had recently taken a sudden and dramatic turn, and it was a miracle that Glenn was sitting across from me.

On September 25, 2001 - exactly one week earlier - Glenn, who had become an Orthopedic Sales Representative with Orthopedic Implants, was in an Operating Room in Beaufort, SC, overseeing a procedure when he suffered a massive heart attack and was rushed to the ER.

He died.

Because he was there - in the hospital - the medical personnel were able to resuscitate and stabilize him. Had he been anywhere else that morning, the outcome would have been different.

Because Beaufort didn't have a cardiac facility, he was flown to North Charleston where the helicopter landed on Charleston Southern University's Soccer Field. From there, an ambulance transported him across the street to Trident Hospital where he was met by some of his family and his priest.

Before he was taken into the hospital, he had the pressing need to speak with his wife and his priest privately. He wanted to tell them what he had experienced.

After being hospitalized, Glenn was discharged to his home. Seven days after his heart attack, Glenn had two things on his mind: thanking the medical transport crew who helped him, and he wanted to visit my mom.

My mother was unconscious as PJ, who had become a Therapeutic Nurse Massage Therapist, lovingly massaged her body. Glenn, however, had a different purpose. He felt compelled to share his experience with us. He was a messenger who had words my mother needed to hear - perhaps it is a message we all need to hear:

"When the time comes - there is no fear - the pain goes away. It is all right to go Home. Everything is going to be OK."

I could hardly hold back the tears, and at that moment, it felt as though the veil that separates Heaven and Earth had grown thin.

Because this was Mr. LePine - a person I'd known most of my life - there is absolutely no doubt in my mind that he left the confines of this earthly life and came back with a mission of relaying this message of peace to my mother and to others who might need to hear it. This gives me chills even now.

Over the years, Glenn has asked why he was able to return when so many others don't get that chance. He feels that he is here, in part, to share the profound message he shared with my mother.

As he held my mother's hand that morning and spoke of his experience, the refrain of the song that was playing when they entered the room still echoed in my mind. Before they left the hospital, I played that song for them.

Oh, What do I know?
I don't know that there are harps in heaven,
Or the process for earning your wings.
I don't know of bright lights at the ends of tunnels,
Or any of those things.
But I know to be absent from this body is to be present with the Lord,
and from what I know of him, that must be pretty good.
What Do I Know by Sara Groves

CHAPTER TWENTY

Mom's Last Breath

It was early Thursday morning, October 4, 2001, and Mom was still hanging on after days of standing at the precipice of eternity. With her eyes shut, it was as though she was staring into another realm through the portal of her soul.

The Oncologist doing his rounds couldn't believe that we were still there. He joked that, once again, Mom surpassed his expectations. He seemed slightly emotional as he turned to leave commenting that he shared in our grief – because she was not just a patient but a friend.

The nurse who had cared for Mom overnight – a nurse none of us had seen before – was finishing her shift but asked to have a word with us. She shared that she lived in the neighborhood across the street from ours, and that she and her family had been praying for Mom and for us.

Strangely, she was on her way to attend a parent/teacher conference at the school where my mother taught for almost 20 years. She was meeting with one of

Mom's closest friends, Mrs. Cindy McIntosh McDowell.

Her replacement was Jan. We met Jan just a few nights earlier and hadn't seen her since.

When we first met her, my sister, Susan, asked Jan what we'd witness when Mom died. We all wanted to be there when the time came.

Jan explained with a complete sense of authority what we would experience in almost a step-by-step way. We later conveyed the details to my brother, Tim, and his wife, Nicole, so that we'd all be aware of what to watch for.

When Jan entered the room, just hours before mom died, we all felt a sense of peace. Even though we had decided that we would not leave mom alone, we heeded her suggestion to leave and have breakfast. She assured us that Mom would still be alive when we returned... and we trusted her.

While Dad, Susan, Tim, and Nicole went to a restaurant, I stayed at the hospital eating the worst canteen vending machine breakfast you could ever imagine.

I returned to the room about 40 minutes later and was surprised to find Jan combing Mom's hair. Mom was propped up by pillows and even though she was not conscious, she looked better than she had in weeks. It was as though the atmosphere of the room had changed...the air was fresher and cooler...and Jan was playing a CD of Pachelbel's *Canon in D*; one of Mom's favorite songs.

Jan did this to give mom some dignity in her final hours and give us a better image by which to remember her.

Seeing this, I broke into tears…and hearing *Canon in D* did NOT help. I was so grateful for this gift – as was the rest of the family when they returned from breakfast.

We were all running on fumes. Dad and Susan decided to go home to shower and rest. Just as they began to leave, the door opened and an attractive 20-something-year-old nurse with blond hair, bright blue eyes, and an effervescent personality entered the room. Her name was Paige.

My dad seemed elated to see her and smiled for the first time in weeks. He acted like he had known her forever…which was odd since none of us knew her at all.

Her spirit was a relief to all of us but especially Dad. For those few moments she was in the room, the wrinkles that had deeply etched their way into his forehead seemed to relax as did his stress-induced furrowed brow.

Paige was the nurse who had completed Mom's discharge paperwork and wheeled her out to the car each time she went home from the hospital.

According to Dad, Mom called Paige her *Shining Star*. Paige seemed to radiate as she told us how, on one occasion, Mom insisted that Paige take a ride in Mom's new car around Downtown Charleston. Paige felt that it was an odd request but she went anyway.

Even though we had been encouraging Mom to let go, it seemed like she was waiting to "see" someone before she parted. Making the connection between

Paige's role in sending mom home in the past, someone suggested that mom might be waiting for Paige. We asked Paige to tell Mom, "It's ok to go," but Paige declined. She had only stopped in to say, "Hello."

Paige went back to work. Dad and Susan went home. Tim, Nicole and I laid down and fell asleep.

About 45 minutes later, the three of us simultaneously woke up — as though an alarm clock had gone off.

Mom's breathing had suddenly changed. This signaled the beginning of the end…just as Jan had explained several nights before.

We called Dad and Susan who had only been home a few minutes. Jan calmly said that they should come back to the hospital but not to worry, Mom would wait for them to return.

It seemed like Dad and Susan were back in a matter of minutes. As soon as they entered the room, Jan commented, "She knows you're here…her breathing just changed again."

We gathered around the bed and shared a mixture of tears and laughter. We were all saying one-liners to lighten the mood. We made fun of the "Medi-Wipe" tissues that the hospital supplied. They were one-ply, if that, and seemed to dissolve when wet…they were awful.

Jan monitored Mom's vital signs and calmly explained what was happening. It was playing out exactly as she said it would. She continually reminded us that Mom's hearing would be the last to go so we repeatedly expressed our love and appreciation to the woman who was so important to each of us.

We cried. We said our goodbyes.

We cried more. We said goodbye again…and again….and again…

It seemed like Mom was still not letting go.

We tried to encourage her by telling her that it was OK to leave.

It felt so odd telling her to let go when that was really the last thing any of us wanted, but there was no coming back from this, and none of us could stand to see her suffer any longer.

As she continued to hold on, the intensity grew. It seemed that things were no longer going according to Jan's "plan," and even Jan seemed a little anxious.

There was a soft knock on the door. As it opened, we were about to tell whoever it was to leave when peace swept over the room – a peace like I had never known. You could almost touch it.

It was Paige…Mom's *Shining Star*…the woman who escorted mom out of the hospital in the past. Something had prompted her to come right then.

Without a word she quietly walked over to the bed, grabbed my Mom's forearm and said, "Mrs. Miller, it's time to go home."

With that, my mother's eyes slightly opened and she released her final breath.

Just like that…

…it was over.

The room fell quiet. Everything was so still.

* * *

After a moment or two, Jan and Paige left. We all began to cry and hug each other. All too soon, the time came to leave, though none of us wanted to.

In the interest of full disclosure, I took everything in the room that was not bolted down.

As Susan and I took a load of goodies to the car, a woman on the elevator commented, "It looks like someone is going home today." Susan and I glanced at each other, nodded, and silently and peacefully confirmed that someone was, indeed, going home.

As we walked out of the hospital just before 1 PM, I heard birds chirping for the first time in what seemed like years. I could not help but think of the lyrics to the hymn Mom chose to open her funeral:

This is my Father's world and to my listening ears all nature sings, and round me rings the music of the spheres.

I have never experienced anything so surreal. Aside from the details of what happened that day, I have a memory that is far more vivid: the feeling in that room.

There is no doubt in my mind that the room was filled with holiness. Something divine and beyond our comprehension was in our midst. As sad as each of us were to lose her, none of us can deny that we encountered God's real angels; Jan and Paige. We were surrounded by, and filled with, God's presence.

These lyrics still resonate deep in my soul...
This is my Father's world, and to my listening ears
All nature sings, and round me rings the music of the spheres.
This is my Father's world: I rest me in the thought

109

Of rocks and trees, of skies and seas;
His hand the wonders wrought.
    This is my Father's world, the birds their carols raise,
The morning light, the lily white, declare their Maker's praise.
This is my Father's world: He shines in all that's fair;
In the rustling grass I hear Him pass;
He speaks to me everywhere.
    This is my Father's world. O let me ne'er forget
That though the wrong seems oft so strong,
God is the ruler yet.
This is my Father's world: the battle is not done:
Jesus Who died shall be satisfied,
And earth and Heav'n be one.
    This is my Father's world, dreaming, I see His face.
I ope' my eyes, and in glad surprise cry,
"The Lord is in this place."
This is my Father's world, from the shining courts above,
The Beloved One, His Only Son,
Came—a pledge of deathless love.
    This is my Father's world, should my heart be ever sad?
The lord is King—let the heavens ring.
God reigns—let the earth be glad.
This is my Father's world. Now closer to Heaven bound,
For dear to God is the earth Christ trod.
No place but is holy ground.
    This is my Father's world. I walk a desert lone.
In a bush ablaze to my wondering gaze
God makes His glory known.
This is my Father's world, a wanderer I may roam
Whate'er my lot, it matters not,
My heart is still at home.

CHAPTER TWENTY-ONE

Grief

Whenever I or people I know experience intense grief, I am mindful of something that was shared with me when my mother passed by a church-family friend, Rosie Soderlund.

When we arrived home from the hospital just after my mom passed, Rosie was cleaning our kitchen because she knew we'd be hosting a number of friends over the next few days.

"Grief is like a cut," she said before explaining:
It bleeds a lot at first and begins to heal slowly - very slowly, but the slightest touch can make it bleed again. Your body redoubles its effort to heal the wound but the scab will occasionally get pulled off, and you'll experience the pain once again.

Then, one day...after some time...you look down and see that somehow the wound has sealed up and it no longer bleeds...but it isn't gone.

You're left with a scar...a permanent reminder that will remain with you for as long as you're in your body.

Another pearl of wisdom she gave me was:
"Without tears, the soul can't have rainbows."

PART FOUR

Small Town Livin'

CHAPTER TWENTY-TWO

Hurricane Hugo

Growing up, many of my neighbors felt more like family than people who just lived in our neighborhood.

Hurricane Hugo - as bad as it was - drew us even closer.

I'll never forget the sound of chainsaws that ran from sun-up to sun-down, the countless hours spent hauling debris, and all the great food we shared together.

In the days leading up to the storm and for many months (or years) that followed, you wouldn't think of passing by a person in need without offering to do what you could to help...and that wasn't limited to just our street. It felt like everyone you saw - regardless of color or creed - was your neighbor.

It was that connection that helped us carry on.

It is too bad that it often takes something devastating to put life into perspective.

The hurricanes, fires, and earthquakes we've seen recently have been awful. I pray that, in the midst of recovering, people might experience the same unifying bonds our neighbors experienced so many years ago -

bonds that continue to this day. Might that be enough to sustain those who've lost everything else.

As *Hurricane Florence* threatened the Charleston area in August-September of this year (2018), I heard some weather reports that compared it to *Hugo*.

I can still remember the night *Hugo* hit: Sept. 22, 1989. I was in tenth grade.

We watched some movies that night; *E.T.* was one of those. As the storm grew stronger, we occasionally stood on our front porch to observe the wind. Eventually, it became too strong, and we had to stay inside. The wind blew so hard that it sent pinecones flying at the side of our house, but they sounded like baseballs.

The power eventually went out, but we had plenty of candles.

At some point, the wind eerily stopped abruptly because we were in the eye of the storm. Everything became still, quiet, and darker than any darkness I had experienced before.

With flashlights, we, along with many of the neighbors, ventured out to assess the damage. Many of the trees were down or leaning and pine straw was EVERYWHERE.

After a few minutes, a neighbor, who had called to check on her family who lived in a neighboring town to our south, yelled outside, "It is starting back up in Hanahan." We had just enough time to get back inside before the wind started back up and when it did, it started back full-strength.

As you can imagine, there was little-to-no sleep for

any of us that night.

The next morning, we *awoke* from what little sleep we did get to the sound of chainsaws. For weeks, whenever the sun was shining, you'd hear the constant sound of chainsaws.

People had to wait in long lines for gas and ice...and water, too...because so many trees had fallen in our water source that it wasn't safe to drink (and that went on for quite a while).

We piled all of the debris near the road. Those piles were immense...and then we had to haul all of it truckload after truckload to a burn site.

BUT...there was a spirit of unity in our community - neighbors helping neighbors...and many of us gathered at a neighbor's home where there was a generator. For the first few nights, we all ate like royalty because everyone had to consume all of the frozen food from our freezers before it went bad.

Because we lived near a power station, we had power relatively quickly but were out of school for at least two weeks, and everyone - and I do mean EVERY single person - worked from sun-up to sun-down.

It isn't something I'd want to do again, but witnessing the generosity of people in our neighborhood and across our country was something I hope I never forget.

CHAPTER TWENTY-THREE

Leaving Rock Hill

Sunday, October 14, 2007, was the day I left Rock Hill, SC, and moved to the Seattle area; Snohomish, WA, to be exact - 5 days, 3027 miles, and 17.5 cups of coffee away. It would have been 18 cups had I not spilled half of one.

In the weeks leading up to my departure, I said many goodbyes - some were easy, some were hard, and some were just plain awkward.

The staff at the church I served did a send-off for me after a staff meeting. A few nights later, the Pastor of the church, Shelton Sanford, had a dinner party for me and the two couples from the church who were closest to me; Kathy and Roland Weathers and John and Linda Godbold. For an appetizer, he prepared Ruth Graham's (Rev. Billy Graham's wife) recipe for baked Brie cheese topped with a delicious and buttery apple, cinnamon, almonds glaze. For dinner, we had Prime Rib and the most deliciously seasoned corn-on-the-cob cooked in the husk on the grill. For dessert, a Dark

Chocolate Cake covered in buttercream and dark chocolate ganache. Delicious.

My friends, John and Linda, hosted the Worship Team for a going-away party at their home. They served all of my favorite foods including Doritos and A1 Sauce as a dip. I know that might sound strange but try it sometime.

I spent a day in Lancaster, SC, where I said goodbye to my grandmother, aunt, uncle, and cousins.

While there, I had dinner with my dear friends, CB and Caroline Mathis. Saying goodbye to those two was difficult. I'd done so much with them over the years.

Singers dating back to 1997 - my first season conducting the *Lancaster Chamber Choir* - sent me away with a notebook filled with notes from nearly every singer who had been in the group during my decade-long tenure.

There was a fun gathering of some of my dearest Winthrop Music Department friends: Kevin Gray, Zeb Roberts, Don Rogers, Mary Ann and Jerry Helton, and Monty Bennett. Monty didn't attend WU but was part of our tribe anyway.

I had dinner with my friend, Amanda Williams. We always laughed so much when together and that night was no exception.

I stopped by to see Wayne & Sharon Goodman and Dale & Susan Dove at their homes in Rock Hill.

I met other Winthrop Friends - Amy Dent, Katherine Farmer, and Shannon Hooker - in Columbia for a goodbye dinner. This was, perhaps, the most fun "going away" as we relived our college days and laughed about performing together, creating Jazz Cats sweatshirts, pushing a car uphill in the rain, levitating, black eyes, "Free Bird," and amazing frisbee tricks.

I made a sweep through my home town of Goose Creek where I saw a number of good friends; Valeri Doughtery, Kirstin Googe, the Mackenzies, the Smoaks, the Esareys, and my high school Band Director, Mr. Jim Haynes.

There were other goodbyes, too, and a few friends who I only had time to visit with on the phone. Among them was Thomas Khoe.

The most awkward goodbye was with another of my closest friends, Barbara Paul. I met her in 1997, and she and I were instant friends. For the next ten years, we went to dinner about once a week. She was older than I was by 40+ years, but age is, as they say, just a number - and that was certainly true for her.

Barbara was the pianist for the *Lancaster Chamber Choir*, a church musician, and a former English teacher. She loved music. More than music, she loved words, and you could tell simply by listening to the joy in her southern lilt when she pronounced certain words or spoke well-crafted phrases:

"that is something up with which I shall not put."

She was wise. I couldn't begin to calculate the amount of advice, wisdom nuggets, and funny stories she shared with me. One source of laughter was a friend of hers who constantly referred to me as Barbara's boyfriend.

A few years before I moved, I came out to her - which was not a surprise to her, of course. She commented, "I knew the moment we met - and I've liked you ever since."

We met at a crucial time in both of our lives. I was starting out my career as a conductor and music educator just after learning that my mother had a terminal case of cancer. Barbara, on the other hand, had recently lost her husband, Sam - also to cancer. We liked each other, enjoyed our times together...and we needed each other. We became a mutual admiration society as well as our own support group.

Over time, we took road trips, and I joined her at family gatherings with her children - all of whom were around 20 years older than I.

There were jokes about how I was trying to get some of their inheritance when she passed away. Although that had never crossed my mind, she did own 400 acres of tree farms on land that was sought after by real estate developers. But the truth is that everyone knew that we had a special bond. Her kids even named me an "Honorary Paul."

Our goodbye began with a candlelight meal which she prepared and served at her house on her most precious china. In our opening conversation, she proclaimed that there would be no tears and no goodbyes.

In all honesty, I'd cried a lot - in private - as the time for my departure neared, but I always maintained a brave face in front of others.

After our meal, we talked for a while - delaying the inevitable...but all too soon the time came for me to leave.

At her door, we hugged, and we both said, "I love you." We usually spoke those words to one another at the end of phone calls or when we parted. I stepped outside, she closed the door, and I as I walked to my car, I turned to look at her through the living room window where she stood watching me - an image that was etched into my memory.

My heart was heavy and even though neither of us cried while together, I think we both shed a tear in the moments that followed.

I knew that that would be my most challenging goodbye, but I still felt a weight surrounding our last moments together. As odd as this may sound, I felt the need to have her blessing or permission to move on - which I didn't really get that night.

On Saturday, the day before I left, my family was with me in Rock Hill. They helped me pack up, we went to eat, and then we said our goodbyes. Everyone except my dad cried, but even he seemed to get choked up as he hugged me and said, "I'm proud of you. Be careful…and in case I don't see you again, have a good life." That might sound a bit fatalistic but the 'have a good life' part was something that his father would often say.

On Sunday morning, I went to church and made an appearance at each of the three church services where I was ceremoniously given a beautiful handmade pottery communion set.

After the services, a reception was held for me. It was a beautiful time. Admittedly, I was on the verge of getting choked up during most of it, but my gratitude for the outpouring of love filled my heart so much that only an occasional tear fell from my eyes.

People gave me beautifully inscribed cards. Some gave me money, and some gave me small tokens of appreciation. One woman who did not attend the service I led, with whom I had a neat connection, gave me the most gorgeous sweater with a note, "On days when you feel alone, wear this and know that you're not."

As part of staff meetings at that church, a pastor would pass out the *Prayer Request Cards* that had been gathered the previous Sunday; 1 or 2 cards per staff member. We'd break into small groups where we'd pray for each other, each other's concerns, each other's ministries, and then we'd pray for those whose cards we had. After our staff meeting, we were to send a card to the person who submitted the prayer request to let them know that we prayed for them and their concerns.

It seemed that week after week, I was handed a card from the same woman - a person who had faced many health battles over the years I was at the church. I sent so many cards to her that I still have her address memorized.

She waited until the reception was wrapping up before she approached me. I can't remember exactly what she said, but she cried and thanked me for the prayers and for being part of her life. She handed me a card and a beautifully wrapped box and told me to open them later. I felt my insides trembling a bit - like a volcano of tears building under pressure, and when we hugged, it was like a release valve and a handful of well-controlled tears seeped out and fell on my cheeks.

I gathered myself together and gave my final goodbyes to the last group of church members - my Worship Team - who all stayed the entire time - waiting until we had a private moment...just us.

Being alone with them as I had been during so many rehearsals was hard. They surrounded me, they laid hands on me, and they prayed for me, for safe travel, and above all, for God's Spirit to guide me and be an ever-present source of comfort and strength then and for the rest of my life. I could feel a lump in my throat, and I was fighting the urge to cry as I felt gratitude mixed with the sense of grief for the loss that I was already experiencing. After the "Amen," we hugged.

As I hugged the last person, I glanced beyond those gathered around me and saw another person who wished to say a proper goodbye.

Walking into the place like she owned the joint - dressed in her formal black with the assistance of a cane was Barbara Paul who had arranged for someone to drive her 40 minutes to the church.

When I saw her, I couldn't contain the emotion any longer and the floodgates opened. I was so overcome that I needed to lean against the wall for a few seconds. Her being there meant the world to me...and it was what I needed - to feel a sense of closure on that leg of my journey.

She wanted to be the last person to bid me farewell...

and she was.

There was a lot of food at the reception, but I didn't eat a bite - I was too busy talking (imagine that: me talking!).

Fortunately, the Food Services Director packed a well-filled to-go box that, like manna from heaven, no matter how much I ate, it always seemed full. As a matter of fact, the first meal I had in Snohomish the night of my arrival (five days later) was food from the reception...and there was still more.

Just before I moved, I read *Walden* by Henry David Thoreau. One passage seemed to resonate deeply with me:

"I went to the woods because I wished to live deliberately, to front only the essential facts of life, and see if I could not learn what it had to teach, and not, when I came to die, discover that I had not lived. I did not wish to live what was not life, living is so dear."

For the first 5-6 months in my new town, I stayed in a lake cabin owned by Randy and Beth Hamlin, members of the church. Interestingly, Beth's father, Pastor Hatlen, had once been the pastor of that church, and he and I share the same birthday.

When I arrived at the cabin for the first time, I was greeted by a sign hanging on the front door that read,

"I went to the woods because I wished to live deliberately."

In that instant, I knew that I was home.

I spent the next day unpacking my truck and getting settled...running to the bank, getting groceries, and practicing the music for Sunday's church service.

As I unpacked, I came across the beautifully wrapped box and card given to me by the woman for whom I had prayed so many times. It brought back a flood of not-too-distant memories that seemingly felt like a lifetime ago. I set the package on the bed to open later.

Over dinner, I opened the card that accompanied the box. It read, "May every blessing that you've prayed for me over the years come back to you tenfold." Inside the box was every card I had sent her over the years.

As simple as that gift was, it was probably the most meaningful...knowing that she had saved all of those cards...that they had served as inspiration and motivation for her...and that she wanted to return all of that to me. That was a real blessing!

That night, I sat quietly in the cabin looking at Lake Roesiger and ate the remaining food from the reception. The lake reflected the gray clouds as a cold mist and stronger-than-normal winds blew. No television, no radio, no internet...no distractions...just me and my thoughts...and a hot cup of tea. I sat there wearing my new sweater - knowing that I wasn't really alone - reflecting on my life, my goodbyes, my trip across the country, and how God had continuously guided and provided.

As I began settling into a new life, I realized that I was, indeed, living deliberately.

Michael Austin Miller

CHAPTER TWENTY-FOUR

Snohomish

I've spent my entire life in small or smallish towns - and I wouldn't have it any other way.

Many neat things happen in small towns. At the beginning of last school year, for instance, I literally saw some local high school boys helping an old lady cross the street.

In recent weeks, I personally witnessed some of the kindness you're not likely to find outside of a small community.

The day before I left for vacation, I took my dog to the spa. Actually, it was the kennel - Paradise Pet Lodge - but because it is the second most expensive line item in my vacation budget and twice as much as the rental car, I call it a spa.

As the dad of a high-maintenance dog, I came with all of Brutus's medications in pillboxes marked with the date and time they were to be administered, and written directions for when and how to give him each of his eyedrops; no sooner than five minutes apart.

I also took 16 individually wrapped bricks of homemade dog food that were labeled with the date and time they were to be given to Brutus…and in case he went on a hunger strike (which he did), I also brought 16 cans of trusty dog food to serve as a substitute.

Of course, I brought the pad that is usually in his crate along with his beloved towel that is shredded beyond recognition, but he'd feel lost without it.

When I arrived at the spa, I left Brutus in the car while I went in to do all the paperwork. People do less paperwork when they are about to have brain surgery.

Anyway, there were two guys there - obviously a couple and obviously, this was their first time leaving their precious puppy at the spa. I heard them tell the woman behind the counter a series of "cute" stories about their dog…and as often as possible, they inserted the comment, "if anything happens, please call us right away - day or night." All I could do was grin while inwardly rolling my eyes and impatiently tapping my foot.

Enough already! I was in a hurry.

Going to the spa takes 20-30 minutes. The return trip, on the other hand, takes 50-60 minutes due to traffic. By the time I finally had my opportunity to impress the employees at the spa with my detailed and pedantic instruction manual on how best to care for my dog, it was after 4:30 PM.

After going through all the paperwork, I noticed that something was missing…my dog's insulin…of all things to forget. This meant that I had to drive all the way home in slow, stop-and-go traffic, get the insulin and return to the spa and then drive in that awful traffic....AGAIN. It was likely that I'd not make it back with the insulin before they closed.

They took Brutus in while I made the trip back home.

In the car - while fuming a bit and frustrated with myself, it occurred to me that I could just go to my vet and get insulin and save about 10 minutes. I called them and they had some! Whew!!

As I paid for the insulin, my Vet sent word to me that he'd be happy to take the insulin to Paradise Pet Lodge after he got off work - to spare me the trip and save all of that time.

It is times like these when I realize how thankful I am to live where I do. On October 14, 2007 (11 years ago tomorrow as I write this), I packed up my truck and moved to Snohomish, WA - a move that, in the words of Robert Frost, "made all the difference" as I've taken the road less traveled.

And yes, I am fully aware that between my dog and me, I am the high-maintenance one.

CHAPTER TWENTY-FIVE
Dynamite

I guess they were selling dynamite this Fourth of July.

Apparently, regular fireworks just aren't good enough for some people.

I can picture an 18-year-old walking up to a fireworks stand:
"Yeah, those M-80s - even though they were created by the U.S. military to simulate artillery fire and combat explosives - they just don't have enough kick for me.
I want something that'll take down a mountain. I want to light it knowing that it'll be the biggest, brightest, loudest, greatest...and probably the last explosion I'll ever see."

PART FIVE

God Winks

CHAPTER TWENTY-SIX

Indelible Marks

1997–1998 was one of the most difficult years of my life. Not only was it the first time I was fully employed as a teacher, my family had just learned of my mother's terminal condition.

Not long after receiving word about Mom's health, one of my dearest friends, Valeri, and her father, Mr. Johnson, came to visit me. He had made a 3-hour road trip on his motorcycle from Goose Creek to see Valeri who taught in a neighboring school district, and to visit relatives in the Lancaster area.

Valeri and I grew up together; same schools, same church, same college. I'd say that she's my oldest friend...but that might get me in trouble. Suffice it to say that she has been a friend of mine longer than anyone else.

Throughout middle and high school, we had "Shin-digs" at her house about once a week. We'd sit in the living room playing music for hours and Mr. Johnson and Valeri's sister, Traci, often joined in.

Though it never seemed like a music lesson, Mr. Johnson taught us so much. In addition to teaching us a number of songs, he taught us how to play keyboard, acoustic guitar, and bass guitar. Most importantly, he taught us the fundamentals of playing with a sense of ensemble – skills I use to this day.

In retrospect, what we did back then was pretty impressive...especially for our age. You should have heard our rendition of *Mansion Over the Hilltop*. I did not realize how special those times were until later in life.

Mr. Johnson was a quiet and youthful man with a quick wit and endearing smile. He had a great laugh and a great heart. Throughout my childhood, he led music at our church – singing and playing guitar and in some cases directing the adult choir. There was something so authentic about what he brought to our church through music. His music came from a deep place and it spoke to me.

As the three of us enjoyed a meal together that night in Lancaster, I began to think that the purpose of the visit was partly for him to check on me. In all honesty, I needed that time with the two of them because I was truly struggling. Instead of being fully engaged in my career as a first-year teacher, my mind was consumed by thoughts about my mother.

For those brief hours, it felt as though everything was right with the world.

Toward the end of the meal, I thanked Mr. Johnson for being one of the earliest musical influences in my life, if not the first, and for being a significant influence on my spiritual life, too.

* * *

I shared a story with them about another experience from my childhood that seemed to propel me toward music and, more importantly, church:

My family was attending the funeral in a small community near Kershaw, South Carolina. During the service, a gentleman with an amazing voice sang the song, *Peace in the Valley.*

He was a tall man with a huge voice. I can remember moving around so that I could see him sing. Not only was his voice powerful…something else seemed to be going on…it was like the barometric pressure in the room had changed.

I felt a presence deep within me − a stirring in my soul.

I had an awareness of God's presence for the first time in my life even though I was very young.

As I expressed my thanks to Mr. Johnson and shared that story with him, I saw someone over his shoulder…a man who seemed to capture my attention, a man whose face reminded me of the man who sang at that funeral so many years before.

I was so distracted that I had to speak with that man.

"Excuse me. I hate to interrupt your dinner. Are you a singer?"

He was.

"Did you, by chance, sing at Louise Fletcher's funeral at Kerwest Baptist Church in the late 70s/early 80s?"

He did.

Right there − in Applebee's − I stood between two booths wherein sat the earliest musical and spiritual influences of my life.

I learned that this man, Gene Ghent, was a teacher and a friend of my mother's sister.

I am not sure if Valeri, Mr. Johnson, or Gene know how significantly they have each impacted my faith and my musicianship, but I am grateful for the indelible mark they have each made on my life.

All of us being in the same place at the same time was beyond coincidence. It was a gift.

In the midst of that hard time in my life, I learned two things:

1) When we find ourselves in need, God sends people to walk along side us to strengthen us, encourage us, and help us renew our faith.

2) In the ministry of church music, you never know when the music you're creating might make an indelible mark on the life of someone listening.

CHAPTER TWENTY-SEVEN

Piano

The day after Halloween is recognized by the church as *All Saints Day*.

As each year goes by, it seems there is an increasing number of names added to my list of Saints I've loved who are now no longer here with us in body.

Thinking about this prompted me to share this story:

Several years ago, my aunt and uncle in Port Townsend told me that their friend, Elvan, wanted to sell her piano and wanted to know if I wanted to buy it.

Elvan and her husband, Mike, a couple who lived near them were both in declining health and had begun the process of downsizing.

Elvan, whose name means "eleven" in Swedish, was the eleventh child in her family. She was the sweetest woman you'd ever meet. Her husband, Mike, on the other hand, was the original "grumpy old man." Elvan said that he never really listened to her play the piano. Instead, he complained that the piano was too loud.

She spoke four languages, having learned French in her 80s. Then, she took a solo trip to France to practice the language. She was an artist, an avid reader, a lover of nature and animals, and an accomplished pianist who owned a Yamaha C3 Grand that was built in 1987.

Not all grand pianos are created equal. The C3 is a highly regarded 6'1" grand piano in Yamaha's Conservatoire series and is designed for professional pianists. They are found on concert stages and in music conservatories around the world.

When I was a kid, I could pick out tunes on the piano by ear. Both of my grandmothers played the piano when they were younger and encouraged me to play. My paternal grandmother even bought an air-organ for her home for me to play when visiting.

Not long after my family moved into our new home in Cherry Hill, my maternal grandmother offered to loan my mother money to buy a piano for our home - which she did. So, in a way, our piano came to us because of my mom's mom.

Before Elvan offered her grand piano to me, she had it appraised. They had planned to sell it to a piano dealer, but since they knew me and knew I played, they asked if I wanted to buy it first. She only wanted $4500.00.

Of course, I wanted to buy it.

I'd always dreamed of having a nice grand piano but the expense - well - great pianos are expensive.

I didn't have the cash immediately on hand at the time so Elvan said that she'd wait until after Christmas to sell it - which would give me some time to save money. She really wasn't in a hurry to get rid of it because she treasured it so.

About a week or so after we made that arrangement, I was surprised to learn that I'd soon receive some money in the mail. Sadly, it was money from my maternal grandmother's estate. She had passed away the previous year. I didn't know how much it would be but when it arrived, there was enough to buy the piano.

I thought it was poetic that my mom's mom - the very person who helped us get our first piano - would help me get my own.

In the meantime, I attended Thanksgiving Day with Mike and Elvan at my aunt's house. Elvan was so excited that I was going to have her piano but also a bit sad to see it go.

After a few drinks, though, Elvan told me that she'd just changed her mind about the price. My heart sank. Her English was pretty good but considering her age and how much we both had to drink, I wasn't sure if I heard her correctly, but I could swear she said that she only wanted $2000.

Because I was unclear, I relayed this information to my aunt and asked if she could verify whether this was accurate and not related to how much alcohol had been consumed.

$2000 it was.

On Tuesday, January 22, 2013, while the piano movers loaded the piano onto the truck, Elvan handed me some paperwork for the piano including the appraisal. When I opened the envelope for the appraisal, I was surprised.

In the top left corner was the date of the appraisal; April 17 - my mother's birthday. Out of 365 days in a year, this piano had been appraised on my mother's birthday.

I knew right then that that piano was meant to be mine, but seeing Elvan cry as the piano left her house was both heartwarming and heartrending.

The next day, January 23, the piano technician arrived to tune the piano. While he worked, I ordered a bouquet of flowers to be delivered to Elvan as a sign of gratitude.

As is often done after a tuning, the tuner played a song to show off his handiwork.

The song he played - of all the pieces in the world - was: *Music Box Dancer.*

That might not mean much to you, but my mom owned the record of that song and it was played countless times in our home; that song was in her Top-5 favorite songs. It was also one of the first songs I learned to play.

It is a song that, when my brother, sister, or I hear it while out and about, we can't help but think about mom. As a matter of fact, hearing that song has prompted me to call or text my siblings something like "I'm at Arby's and *Music Box Dancer* came on. It made me think of mom and of the two of you. Love you both so much!"

As the piano tuner continued to play, it occurred to me that that day, Jan. 23, also happened to be the date of my parents' wedding anniversary.

Twenty months later, on November 27, 2014 - Thanksgiving Day - my uncle went to Mike and Elvan's to start a fire in their wood stove (which had become part of his daily routine) and found Elvan "sleeping" in a living room recliner. She had passed away in her sleep.

Just 22 days later, on December 19, my uncle found Mike "sleeping" in the recliner.

Several of Elvan's paintings now hang in my home. A stained-glass lamp of hers sits atop "our" piano. I turn it on each time I sit down to play and it reminds me:

whether we know it or not - whether we believe it or not - we are constantly surrounded by a cloud of witnesses.

My mom is there along with her mom who bought the piano for me. My dad's mom is there along with others I've loved who are now in spirit.

Elvan is there, too, listening and smiling with every note...and I think Mike's around here somewhere complaining about the piano being too loud.

CHAPTER TWENTY-EIGHT

Faith Can Move Mountains

On July 16, 2005, I was traveling back to Charlotte, NC, from California after attending a worship conference. My first flight landed in Denver. I rushed to the gate for my next and final flight home just in time to hear that the flight had been delayed an hour. This gave me a chance to relax and eat.

I couldn't wait to get home because my family was coming from Charleston to stay with me that night in order to celebrate my birthday the next day.

I've learned to go with the flow when traveling. Just a few weeks earlier, I had taken a trip to Romania where I experienced one delay after another, but on this particular day, the tension escalated dramatically when the flight was delayed again...and then again.

I was keeping my family in the loop, but by that time, I knew that they would arrive at my home long before I would.

After nearly 3 hours of waiting, it was announced that our flight had been cancelled.

Everyone was frustrated, flustered, and furious...in short, tempers were flaring.

Michael Austin Miller

Though I tried to remain calm, my level of anxiety began to rise - not just because of the cancelled flight, but because of all the yelling and cursing that was going on.

"I'm gonna have someone's job over this," one woman angrily yelled. Based solely on her appearance and rudeness, I figured that this was probably her first time out of the back-woods. She did not need someone's job, she needed dentures.

After waiting for 40 minutes there were still 5 or 6 people in front of me. Those in the long line behind me seemed to be losing their minds.

For whatever reason, I had just taken my small, tan, leather-bound bible that had traveled around the world with me out of my carry-on bag when something came over me…my calm presence abruptly changed.

I turned around toward the crowd, raised my bible above my head and slapped it hard. It sounded like a cannon.

Everything and everyone stopped.

Like a boulder hurled into a pond, you could almost see the sound and shock waves move throughout the room.

I felt like Gandalf in *Lord of the Rings*, when he struck the ground with his staff yelling, "You shall not pass!!!"

In an equally authoritative voice, I said, "You folks need to calm down! A few weeks ago, I was in Romania working with people who live in a city dump…and we're all upset because we can't get on a plane??? Put it in perspective, people."

My outburst completely surprised me…but everyone

seemed to come back to their senses and the entire area became eerily quiet.

A woman in her 70s who stood behind me patted me on the shoulder and thanked me. She and her 25+ year old grandson, Chris, were flying home to Charlotte, too. I explained that I was also upset because my family was on their way to my house...that the next day was my birthday...and that I really needed to be at church the next morning.

"You can always miss church...but you need to see your family," she said.

I explained that I worked for the church. With a twinkle in her eye and a chuckle in her voice, she hollered to the clerks behind the counter, "Y'all need to get the preacher to church."

Her comment seemed to get the ball rolling so I didn't tell anyone that I wasn't a preacher.

Her name was Goldi - a name that perfectly fit this sprightly, white-haired woman, whose smile and laugh would shimmer in any room.

After talking with the clerk, I learned that my best option was a flight that would arrive at Washington D.C.'s Dulles Airport at 1:37 AM. From there I would arrive in Charlotte around 11 AM. It would be too late for church but at least I would see my family.

As I said goodbye to Goldi, she asked me to wait a moment - which I did impatiently. I knew that my plane was already boarding. She informed me that she and Chris were going to fly to D.C. with me and that they would drive me home.

She continued, "You have to be in church...and you need to see your family...it is your birthday, after all!"

I was confused and surprised. She later explained that they lived in Mooresville, NC - a town about an hour north of my home - so it was not a major inconvenience for them.

The three of us were making our way to the other concourse when a woman driving a handicapped cart noticed the panicked look on our faces as well as Goldi's age. She drove us to our next gate. As we rode on the cart, Chris said, "We need to rent a car."

I looked down and noticed something like a bookmark sticking out of the bible that I still carried in my hand. It was a rental car brochure. Honestly, I do not know how that got there. Regardless, he took it and made the reservation.

We landed around 1:45 AM and waited for luggage that never came. After completing lost-luggage paperwork, a shuttle took us to a rental car lot. We finally left the airport just before 3 AM. I was doing the math all along knowing that it did not seem possible for me to make the 9:25 worship service.

About a decade earlier, I was an assistant instructor for the Mooresville High School Band. In trying to make connections with Goldi and Chris, I mentioned the only family I could still remember; the Marions. Randy Marion owned a Chevrolet dealership in the small town of Mooresville, and the family had been heavily involved with the band.

Goldi and Chris didn't just know them, they had recently seen them. As it turned out, Chris was related to Ben Mynatt who owned Mynatt Chevrolet - another Chevrolet dealership in our area.

Chris drove, and though it was not his fault, we found every single possible road-construction detour between D.C. and Mooresville. It is important to note that Chris would not speed. I kept wishing he'd floor it but he obeyed the law.

Around 7:00 am, we were still about 3 hours away but I held out hope that, somehow, I'd make the 9:25 worship service. I called the pastor of the church to update him on my status. He encouraged me not to worry about missing church.

I seemed to lose track of time and after stopping at an interstate exit in Mooresville, where Goldi and Chris met a family member who took them home, I took the wheel and continued to Rock Hill, SC - over an hour away. I did go about 5 miles over the speed limit, but I still cannot account for how quick the trip was.

I felt like I had entered the "Twilight Zone" because, from that point on, I felt like I had entered a time warp and miraculously, I arrived in the worship hall at 9:15.

As I walked onto the platform to lead worship, I saw my family who came to church despite my absence. To say that they were surprised would be an understatement.

About mid-way through the service it dawned on me that I was still wearing the clothes from the day before, my hair was a mess, and I had not brushed my teeth.

Oh well.

At the end of the service, I shared with the congregation what happened. When I finished my tale, they broke out in thunderous applause. One of the pastors offered a prayer of thanksgiving in which he quoted the passage about the faith of a mustard seed moving mountains. In a very real way, this trip taught me the truth in that passage.

My family and I celebrated my return...and my birthday...over lots of smiles, laughs, and a few tears.

About a month later I visited my Grandma who lived in Kershaw, SC.

She asked, "Did someone drive you home from Washington D.C.?"

Just a few days earlier, a visitor sat next to my Grandma at church. The visitor shared a story about how she and her grandson drove someone home from Washington so that he would be at church and with his family on his birthday.

The visitor was Goldi and somehow, through the course of her story, my Grandma determined that the one she drove home was me. It is important to know that Kershaw is over two hours away from Mooresville.

I am not sure how any of this happened but I am very certain that it was a case of divine intervention and certainly was an experience where I felt that my faith had moved mountains - or altered time - or something.

CLOSING

Thank you for taking time to read this book. I hope you enjoyed these stories.

As I wrote in the *Introduction*, "we learn about ourselves and our place in this world by the stories we hear, the stories we retell, the stories we craft and share, but most importantly, the stories we tell ourselves *about* ourselves." It is so true.

Stories *are* treasures.

While working on this project, I learned that stories allow me - or call me - to embrace my highest and best self, and I think that is ultimately the reason I tell and write stories.

Through stories, I can create a world where I meet the best parts of who I am. Seeing what *could* be gives me an even greater, more vivid image of the life I wish to live.

Again, I do hope that you experienced an occasional chuckle, chill, or tear. More than anything, I hope these stories have reminded you of your own stories.

If you enjoyed reading this, please take a moment to give it a favorable 5-star review on Amazon.com

In praise of Miller's first book, *Can I Tell You a Story?*

 - reviews from <u>Amazon.com</u>.

True stories...love them all! Michael has a special gift of putting memories in word form better than anyone. As I began reading this, I was seriously laughing out loud. Our family memories good, fun, or even sad are what makes our family so amazing. Thank you for writing our history. — Susan Still

This will make you laugh and cry and want to join the family. Michael Austin Miller's writing is beautiful and evocative of the kind of family stories we all have, but struggle to tell. I promise whatever family you came from you will experience characters you will love and wish you could meet. Or have a meal with. Or cry with. Give yourself a treat and read this book. — Ron Anderson

A must read! This is funny! —Phyllis Bruner

Hilarious and heartwarming! The power went out a few weeks back and I read M. Miller's book by the light of a lantern, which seems fitting, as his delightful tales of family and the antics of his church community have a timeless quality. Reminiscent of Garrison Keillor, Michael Miller's stories will make you laugh out loud, shed a tear, and warm your heart like hot cocoa on a winter's night. I'd love to see more from this author! — Suzanne Macpherson

Great read! I laughed, I cried, I got chills. I really enjoyed these varied stories, many of which reminded me of my own formative years in the South. — Cheryl Vines

This book provided me with memories from my own childhood. I really enjoyed reading this book. When I came to pages 112 and 113 and found the lyrics to "This Is My Father's World," I was taken back to the past. Standing next to my grandmother as a child at our church service and looking up at her as she sang that hymn and thinking she had the most beautiful voice in the world. This is my favorite hymn of all time. Thank you, Michael for sharing it. — Kristen Werner

This is one of those books that warms the heart. It's funny, charming and so fun

to read. I've read several parts Over and over. Delightful! — Amazon reviewer

A great book of humor, faith, and unexpected human connections. Michael Miller has put it all out there in a very touching collection of personal life stories. I know Michael well and have always enjoyed his humor and wit while telling stories. He seems to have this warm and infectious pull that brings people to him with ties from other times and places. I highly recommend reading this book- his stories will draw you in and walk away with appreciation for those in our lives- past, present and future. — Angie Godfrey

Delightful. I thoroughly enjoyed this book. Michael Miller is a gifted storyteller with chapters that will make you laugh and others that will make you cry. I'm looking forward to what's next from this author. — Julie M. Stephenson

Best book of the year! I know the author as a talented musician who occasionally told stories. This book proves he is both a talented musician and author. This embellished autobiography will have you in stitches one minute and tears the next. His sensitivity and sense of humor shine throughout this work. — Betty Bennett

A feel-good read. The stories in this book are heartwarming and filled with emotion, and made me chuckle. Miller's writing is real and from the heart—a definite good read. — Melissa Marzolf

Must read. This book will make you laugh and cry. I loved every chapter. — Manuela S.

Our family stories, like Miller's stories, are about the triumphs, tragedies, and everyday occurrences that are memorable and worth telling, re-telling and sharing. Some of our family's stories are even true, though in the re-telling they do seem to change a bit over time by who is telling them.
One of my families is the family of music, which I share with Michael. It is a deep and meaningful family. I have watched Michael stand on his director's podium each week and prod, encourage and draw beauty from a disparate group of voices. One of his most effective tools in this exercise is his craft of story telling.

Telling stories that remind us of history, context, dreams and reminder of what we are attempting.
"Can I Tell You a Story?" is a wonderful telling of a large part of who Michael is. It provides a glimpse of his story. How wonderful that he has shared his stories. Who knows what they will become on their re-telling? — T. H. Coble

A quick and easy read with plenty of chuckles and tears. I love how Micheal uses his life stories to help and teach others. — S. Britton

Michael Miller brings the wonderful, beautiful, craziness of family to life in his book, "Can I Tell You a Story?" He will bring tears of laughter, joy, and heartache as you read his accounts of growing up in South Carolina, and his life in Washington. Enjoy. — KarelAnne

Full of heart, humor, and wisdom. These stories are the kind you love to hear around a campfire and around the family dinner table. They are the stories of family and community and good people with the best of intentions, despite sometimes falling short of the mark. And when they do fall short, the results can be hilarious. I nearly split a gut laughing at some of these tales. Yet they are also full of thought-provoking ideas that can keep you musing for days. For a refreshing escape, pick up a copy. — Wendy Hinman

Childhood memories! Delightful! Miller is a master storyteller! This book is a wonderful and easy read! As the reader, you can relate to these fun and adventurous tales of childhood! Loved every minute of it! Thank you! — Amazon reviewer

A slice of Americana from a most warm and wonderful writer. "Can I Tell You a Story?" is my go-to book when I am waiting in line or sitting waiting for an appointment. I've read the book so many times, know the stories so well, but I just never tire of reading Michael's writings about childhood, adulthood, family, life, death, and things we've all experienced. He has wit and warmth and ultimately his stories really are about relationships and connections with people - - which he cares deeply about. Bring on a second book of stories, Michael! — Beth Hamlin

Can I Tell You a Story?

* * *

Michael tells a great story. Reading this book reminded me of similar fond memories in my own life. The humor was fantastic, and the section dedicated to his mom was really powerful. I cannot recommend this one enough. This is an EASY 5 stars. — Raymond Owens

We should all be so gifted! Michael Miller's recollections of the events and people who have shared his life supply his readers with abundant laughter, tears, and honesty, which in turn let flow nostalgia from the faucets of their own lives. If only we could all be so creative and talented as he is in making us laugh and cry with the characterization of his family and friends and of himself as well. — Linda Vaughan

A book very much worth reading! "Can I tell you a story?" Yes, and I'm so glad you did!
It's not often that I get a chance to step back from the hustle-bustle of life, take a cozy chair, and read for pleasure. Knowing this author/composer/conductor personally, I was compelled to slam on the brakes and do just that with this book! Michael is a gifted story-teller who has a way of drawing you into his experiences; you feel the pain and suffering, the humility, the irony, the bust-a-gut zany humor, but mostly you feel the underlying life-theme of love, as your own. It was touching and familiar in a way that I can't put into words. It just is. This book is a treasure trove of memories and observations worth sharing! My only quibble is that I need more of them to read and reflect on! — Kathleen Alexander

ABOUT THE AUTHOR

Photo: Kerri Rundle, *Radiant Photography by Kerri*

Michael Austin Miller grew up in Goose Creek, SC - a suburb of Charleston. After attending Winthrop University in Rock Hill, SC, where he studied music, he became a music teacher, choral conductor, and church musician.

Today, he lives in Snohomish, WA, a suburb of Seattle. He continues his work as a church musician and is the *Artistic Director* and *Conductor* of the Bainbridge Chorale on Bainbridge Island; a ferry ride across the Puget Sound from Seattle.

He enjoys composing music for choirs. Some of his music has been published by *Oxford University Press* and *MorningStar Music Publishers*.

He tries to find time each day to create something whether that be composing music or writing prose. When it comes to writing, he enjoys crafting fictional short stories, non-fiction accounts of real-life experiences, and humorous bits - mostly about his life and the lives of his fun and funny family.

For more information, visit www.MichaelAustinMiller.com, or email MichaelAustinMiller@gmail.com.

Michael Austin Miller's Second Book

Homespun Humor and Half-true Tales is a collection of short stories based around a fictional town in the foothills of the Cascade Mountains; a town named Snow Valley.

Like many small towns, Snow Valley has its own myths, folklore, and tales of heroic legends, quirky characters, and unique traditions.

These stories are told from the perspective of a young man who returned to his hometown after college with fresh eyes to see that normal everyday life in Snow Valley is anything but *normal*. With a deep love for his town and its people, he has become the town's self-appointed historian, and he loves sharing stories about the town's interesting past.

A few words to those visiting Snow Valley for the first time: Take some time to enjoy a few of the many town events, parades, and celebrations. You can get just about everything you might need - including lingerie -

at Tabby's Grocery Store, and don't tell Miss Hilda any secrets you don't want everyone in town to know.

One last thing: if you come expecting snow in Snow Valley, you'll probably be disappointed.

Available now on <u>Amazon.com</u>.

For more information,
visit <u>www.MichaelAustinMiller.com</u>
or email <u>MichaelAustinMiller@gmail.com</u>

54527705R00093

Made in the USA
Columbia, SC
01 April 2019